J. Lesslie Hall

Beowulf

An Anglo-Saxon Epic Poem

J. Lesslie Hall

Beowulf
An Anglo-Saxon Epic Poem

ISBN/EAN: 9783337091583

Printed in Europe, USA, Canada, Australia, Japan

Cover: Foto ©Andreas Hilbeck / pixelio.de

More available books at **www.hansebooks.com**

BEOWULF,

AN ANGLO-SAXON EPIC POEM,

TRANSLATED

FROM THE HEYNE-SOCIN TEXT

BY

JNO: LESSLIE HALL,

PROFESSOR OF ENGLISH AND HISTORY IN THE COLLEGE
OF WILLIAM AND MARY.

(Presented to the Board of University Studies of the Johns Hopkins University for the Degree of Doctor of Philosophy.)

BOSTON, U.S.A.:

D. C. HEATH & CO., PUBLISHERS.

1892.

TYPOGRAPHY BY J. S. CUSHING & CO., BOSTON, U.S.A.

PRESSWORK BY BERWICK & SMITH, BOSTON, U.S.A.

TO

My Wife.

CONTENTS.

Contents.

PREFACE.

THE present work is a modest effort to reproduce approximately, in modern measures, the venerable epic, Beowulf. *Approximately*, I repeat ; for a very close reproduction of Anglo-Saxon verse would, to a large extent, be prose to a modern ear.

The Heyne-Socin text and glossary have been closely followed. Occasionally a deviation has been made, but always for what seemed good and sufficient reason. The translator does not aim to be an editor. Once in a while, however, he has added a conjecture of his own to the emendations quoted from the criticisms of other students of the poem.

This work is addressed to two classes of readers. From both of these alike the translator begs sympathy and co-operation. The Anglo-Saxon scholar he hopes to please by adhering faithfully to the original. The student of English literature he aims to interest by giving him, in modern garb, the most ancient epic of our race. This is a bold and venturesome undertaking ; and yet there must be some students of the Teutonic past willing to follow even a daring guide, if they may read in modern phrases of the sorrows of Hrothgar, of the prowess of Beowulf, and of the feelings that stirred the hearts of our forefathers in their primeval homes.

In order to please the larger class of readers, a regular cadence has been used, a measure which, while retaining the essential characteristics of the original, permits the reader to see ahead of him in reading.

Perhaps every Anglo-Saxon scholar has his own theory as to how Beowulf should be translated. Some have given us prose versions of what we believe to be a great poem. Is it any reflection on our honored Kemble and Arnold to say that their translations fail to show a layman that Beowulf is justly called our first *epic* ? Of those translators who have used verse, several have written from what would seem a mistaken point of view. Is it proper, for instance, that the grave and solemn speeches of Beowulf and Hrothgar be put in ballad measures, tripping lightly and airily along? Or, again, is it fitting that the rough martial music of Anglo-Saxon verse be interpreted to us in the smooth measures of modern blank verse? Do we hear what has been beautifully called "the clanging tread of a warrior in mail"?

Of all English translations of Beowulf, that of Professor Garnett alone gives any adequate idea of the chief characteristics of this great Teutonic epic.

The measure used in the present translation is believed to be as near a reproduction of the original as modern English affords. The cadences closely resemble those used by Browning in some of his most striking poems. The four stresses of the Anglo-Saxon verse are retained, and as much thesis and anacrusis is allowed as is consistent with a regular cadence. Alliteration has been used to a large extent; but it was thought that modern ears would hardly tolerate it on every line. End-rhyme has been used occasionally; internal rhyme, sporadically. Both have some warrant in Anglo-Saxon poetry. (For end-rhyme, see 1 53, 1 54; for internal rhyme, 2 21, 6 40.)

What Gummere [1] calls the "rime-giver" has been studiously kept; *viz.*, the first accented syllable in the second half-verse always carries the alliteration; and the last accented syllable alliterates only sporadically. Alternate alliteration is occasionally used as in the original. (See 7 61, 8 5.)

No two accented syllables have been brought together, except occasionally after a cæsural pause. (See 2 19 and 12 1.) Or, scientifically speaking, Sievers's C type has been avoided as not consonant with the plan of translation. Several of his types, however, constantly occur; *e.g.* A and a variant ($\angle \times \mid \angle \times$) ($\angle \times \times \mid \angle \times$); B and a variant ($\times \angle \mid \times \angle$) ($\times \times \angle \mid \times \angle$); a variant of D ($\angle \times \mid \angle \times \times$); E ($\angle \times \times \mid \angle$). Anacrusis gives further variety to the types used in the translation.

The parallelisms of the original have been faithfully preserved. (*E.g.*, 1 16 and 1 17: "Lord" and "Wielder of Glory"; 1 30, 1 31, 1 32; 2 12 and 2 13; 2 27 and 2 28; 3 5 and 3 6.) Occasionally, some loss has been sustained; but, on the other hand, a gain has here and there been made.

The effort has been made to give a decided flavor of archaism to the translation. All words not in keeping with the spirit of the poem have been

---

[1] Handbook of Poetics, page 175, 1st edition.

avoided. Again, though many archaic words have been used, there are none, it is believed, which are not found in standard modern poetry.

With these preliminary remarks, it will not be amiss to give an outline of the story of the poem.

THE STORY.

Hrothgar, king of the Danes, or Scyldings, builds a great mead-hall, or palace, in which he hopes to feast his liegemen and to give them presents. The joy of king and retainers is, however, of short duration. Grendel, the monster, is seized with hateful jealousy. He cannot brook the sounds of joyance that reach him down in his fen-dwelling near the hall. Oft and anon he goes to the joyous building, bent on direful mischief. Thane after thane is ruthlessly carried off and devoured, while no one is found strong enough and bold enough to cope with the monster. For twelve years he persecutes Hrothgar and his vassals.

Over sea, a day's voyage off, Beowulf, of the Geats, nephew of Higelac, king of the Geats, hears of Grendel's doings and of Hrothgar's misery. He resolves to crush the fell monster and relieve the aged king. With fourteen chosen companions, he sets sail for Dane-land. Reaching that country, he soon persuades Hrothgar of his ability to help him. The hours that elapse before night are spent in beer-drinking and conversation. When Hrothgar's bedtime comes he leaves the hall in charge of Beowulf, telling him that never before has he given to another the absolute wardship of his palace. All retire to rest, Beowulf, as it were, sleeping upon his arms.

Grendel comes, the great march-stepper, bearing God's anger. He seizes and kills one of the sleeping warriors. Then he advances towards Beowulf. A fierce and desperate hand-to-hand struggle ensues. No arms are used, both combatants trusting to strength and hand-grip. Beowulf tears Grendel's shoulder from its socket, and the monster retreats to his den, howling and yelling with agony and fury. The wound is fatal.

The next morning, at early dawn, warriors in numbers flock to the hall Heorot, to hear the news. Joy is boundless. Glee runs high. Hrothgar and his retainers are lavish of gratitude and of gifts.

Grendel's mother, however, comes the next night to avenge his death. She is furious and raging. While Beowulf is sleeping in a room somewhat apart

Preface.

from the quarters of the other warriors, she seizes one of Hrothgar's favorite counsellors, and carries him off and devours him. Beowulf is called. Determined to leave Heorot entirely purified, he arms himself. and goes down to look for the female monster. After traveling through the waters many hours, he meets her near the sea-bottom. She drags him to her den. There he sees Grendel lying dead. After a desperate and almost fatal struggle with the woman, he slays her, and swims upward in triumph, taking with him Grendel's head.

Joy is renewed at Heorot. Congratulations crowd upon the victor. Hrothgar literally pours treasures into the lap of Beowulf; and it is agreed among the vassals of the king that Beowulf will be their next liegelord.

Beowulf leaves Dane-land. Hrothgar weeps and laments at his departure.

When the hero arrives in his own land, Higelac treats him as a distinguished guest. He is the hero of the hour.

Beowulf subsequently becomes king of his own people, the Geats. After he has been ruling for fifty years, his own neighborhood is wofully harried by a fire-spewing dragon. Beowulf determines to kill him. In the ensuing struggle both Beowulf and the dragon are slain. The grief of the Geats is inexpressible. They determine, however, to leave nothing undone to honor the memory of their lord. A great funeral-pyre is built, and his body is burnt. Then a memorial-barrow is made, visible from a great distance, that sailors afar may be constantly reminded of the prowess of the national hero of Geatland.

The poem closes with a glowing tribute to his bravery, his gentleness, his goodness of heart, and his generosity.

It is the devout desire of this translator to hasten the day when the story of Beowulf shall be as familiar to English-speaking peoples as that of the Iliad. Beowulf is our first great epic. It is an epitomized history of the life of the Teutonic races. It brings vividly before us our forefathers of pre-Alfredian eras, in their love of war, of sea, and of adventure.

My special thanks are due to Professors Francis A. March and James A. Harrison, for advice, sympathy, and assistance.

J. L. HALL.

WILLIAMSBURG, VA., Nov. 1, 1891.

ABBREVIATIONS USED IN THE NOTES.

B. = Bugge. C. = Cosijn. Gr. = Grein. Grdvtg. = Grundtvig. H. = Heyne. H. and S. = Harrison and Sharp. H.-So. = Heyne-Socin. K. = Kemble. Kl. = Kluge. M. = Müllenhoff. R. = Rieger. S. = Sievers. Sw. = Sweet. t. B. = ten Brink. Th. = Thorpe. W. = Wülcker.

BIBLIOGRAPHY OF TRANSLATIONS.

Arnold, Thomas. — Beowulf. A heroic poem of the eighth century. London, 1876. With English translation. Prose.

Botkine, L. — Beowulf. Épopée Anglo-Saxonne. Havre, 1877. First French translation. Passages occasionally omitted.

Conybeare, J. J. — Illustrations of Anglo-Saxon Poetry. London, 1826. Full Latin translation, and some passages translated into English blank-verse.

Ettmüller, L. — Beowulf, stabreimend übersetzt. Zürich, 1840.

Garnett, J. M. — Beowulf: an Anglo-Saxon Poem, and the Fight at Finnsburg. Boston, 1882. An accurate line-for-line translation, using alliteration occasionally, and sometimes assuming a metrical cadence.

Grein, C. W. M. — Dichtungen der Angelsachsen, stabreimend übersetzt. 2 Bde. Göttingen, 1857-59.

Grion, Giusto. — Beovulf, poema epico anglo-sassone del VII. secolo, tradotto e illustrato. Lucca, 1883. First Italian translation.

Grundtvig, N. F. S. — Bjowulfs Drape. Copenhagen, 1820.

Heyne, M. — A translation in iambic measures. Paderborn, 1863.

Kemble, J. M. — The Anglo-Saxon Poems of Beowulf, the Traveller's Song, and the Battle of Finnsburg. London, 1833. The second edition contains a prose translation of Beowulf.

Leo, H. — Ueber Beowulf. Halle, 1839. Translations of extracts.

Lumsden, H. W. — Beowulf, translated into modern rhymes. London, 1881. Ballad measures. Passages occasionally omitted.

Sandras, G. S. — De carminibus Cædmoni adjudicatis. Paris, 1859. An extract from Beowulf, with Latin translation.

Schaldmose, F. — Beowulf og Scopes Widsith, to Angelsaxiske Digte. Copenhagen, 1847.

Simrock, K. — Beowulf. Uebersetzt und erläutert. Stuttgart und Augsburg, 1859. Alliterative measures.

Thorkelin, G. J. — De Danorum rebus gestis secul. III. et IV. poema Danicum dialecto Anglosaxonica. Havniæ, 1815. Latin translation.

Thorpe, B. — The Anglo-Saxon Poems of Beowulf, the Scôp or Gleeman's Tale, and the Fight at Finnsburg. Oxford, 1855. English translation in short lines, generally containing two stresses.

Wackerbarth, A. D. — Beowulf, translated into English verse. London, 1849.

Wickberg, R. — Beowulf, en fornengelek hjeltedikt, öfersatt. Westevvik. First Swedish translation.

von Wolzogen, H. — Beowulf, in alliterative measures. Leipzig.

Zinsser, G. — Der Kampf Beowulfs mit Grendel. Jahresbericht of the Realschule at Forbach, 1881.

GLOSSARY OF PROPER NAMES.

[The figures refer to the divisions of the poem in which the respective names occur. The large figures refer to fitts; the small, to lines in the fitts.]

Ælfhere. — A kinsman of Wiglaf. — 36 3.

Æschere. — Confidential friend of King Hrothgar. Elder brother of Yrmenlaf. Killed by Grendel. — 21 3; 30 89.

Beanstan. — Father of Breca. — 9 26.

Beowulf. — Son of Scyld, the founder of the dynasty of Scyldings. Father of Healfdene, and grandfather of Hrothgar. — 1 18; 2 1.

Beowulf. — The hero of the poem. Sprung from the stock of Geats, son of Ecgtheow. Brought up by his maternal grandfather Hrethel, and figuring in manhood as a devoted liegeman of his uncle Higelac. A hero from his youth. Has the strength of thirty men. Engages in a swimming-match with Breca. Goes to the help of Hrothgar against the monster Grendel. Vanquishes Grendel and his mother. Afterwards becomes king of the Geats. Late in life attempts to kill a fire-spewing dragon, and is slain. Is buried with great honors. His memorial mound. — 6 26; 7 2; 7 9; 9 3; 9 8; 12 28; 12 43; 23 1, etc.

Breca. — Beowulf's opponent in the famous swimming-match. — 9 8; 9 19; 9 21; 9 22.

Brondings. — A people ruled by Breca. — 9 23.

Brosinga mene. — A famous collar once owned by the Brosings. — 19 7.

Cain. — Progenitor of Grendel and other monsters. — 2 56; 20 11.

Dæghrefn. — A warrior of the Hugs, killed by Beowulf. — 35 40.

Danes. — Subjects of Scyld and his descendants, and hence often called Scyldings. Other names for them are Victory-Scyldings, Honor-Scyldings, Armor-Danes, Bright-Danes, East-Danes, West-Danes, North-Danes, South-Danes, Ingwins, Hrethmen. — 1 1; 2 1; 3 2; 5 14; 7 1, etc.

Ecglaf. — Father of Unferth, who taunts Beowulf. — 9 1.

Ecgtheow. — Father of Beowulf, the hero of the poem. A widely-known Wægmunding warrior. Marries Hrethel's daughter. After slaying Heatholaf, a Wylfing, he flees his country. — 7 3; 5 6; 8 4.

Ecgwela. — A king of the Danes before Scyld. — 25 60.

xiii

Elan. — Sister of Hrothgar, and probably wife of Ongentheow, king of the Swedes. — 2 10.

Eagle Cape. — A promontory in Geat-land, under which took place Beowulf's last encounter. — 41 87.

Eadgils. — Son of Ohthere and brother of Eanmund. — 34 2.

Eanmund. — Son of Ohthere and brother of Eadgils. The reference to these brothers is vague, and variously understood. Heyne supposes as follows: Raising a revolt against their father, they are obliged to leave Sweden. They go to the land of the Geats; with what intention, is not known, but probably to conquer and plunder. The Geatish king, Heardred, is slain by one of the brothers, probably Eanmund. — 36 10; 31 54 to 31 60; 33 66 to 34 6.

Eofor. — A Geatish hero who slays Ongentheow in war, and is rewarded by Hygelac with the hand of his only daughter. — 41 18; 41 48.

Eormenric. — A Gothic king, from whom Hama took away the famous Brosinga mene. — 19 9.

Eomær. — Son of Offa and Thrytho, king and queen of the Angles. — 28 69.

Finn. — King of the North-Frisians and the Jutes. Marries Hildeburg. At his court takes place the horrible slaughter in which the Danish general, Hnæf, fell. Later on, Finn himself is slain by Danish warriors. — 17 18; 17 30; 17 44; 18 4; 18 23.

Fin-land. — The country to which Beowulf was driven by the currents in his swimming-match. — 10 22.

Fitela. — Son and nephew of King Sigemund, whose praises are sung in XIV. — 14 42; 14 53.

Folcwalda. — Father of Finn. — 17 38.

Franks. — Introduced occasionally in referring to the death of Higelac. — 19 19; 40 21; 40 24.

Frisians. — A part of them are ruled by Finn. Some of them were engaged in the struggle in which Higelac was slain. — 17 20; 17 42; 17 52; 40 21.

Freaware. — Daughter of King Hrothgar. Married to Ingeld, a Heathobard prince. — 29 60; 30 32.

Froda. — King of the Heathobards, and father of Ingeld. — 29 62.

Garmund. — Father of Offa. — 28 71.

Geats, Geatmen. — The race to which the hero of the poem belongs. Also called Weder-Geats, or Weders, War-Geats, Sea-Geats. They are ruled by Hrethel, Hæthcyn, Higelac, and Beowulf. — 4 7; 7 4; 10 45; 11 8; 27 14; 28 8.

Gepids. — Named in connection with the Danes and Swedes. — 35 34.

Grendel. — A monster of the race of Cain. Dwells in the fens and moors. Is furiously envious when he hears sounds of joy in Hrothgar's palace. Causes the king untold agony for years. Is finally conquered by Beowulf, and dies of his wound. His hand and arm are hung up in Hrothgar's hall Heorot. His head is cut off by Beowulf when he goes down to fight with Grendel's mother. — 2 50; 3 1; 3 13; 8 19; 11 17; 12 2; 13 27; 15 3.

Guthlaf. — A Dane of Hnæf's party. — 18 24.

Half-Danes. — Branch of the Danes to which Hnæf belonged. — 17 19.

Halga. — Surnamed the Good. Younger brother of Hrothgar. — 2 9.

Hama. — Takes the Brosinga mene from Eormenric. — 19 7.

Hæreth. — Father of Higelac's queen, Hygd. — 28 39; 29 18.

Hæthcyn. — Son of Hrethel and brother of Higelac. Kills his brother Herebeald accidentally. Is slain at Ravenswood, fighting against Ongentheow. — 34 43; 35 23; 40 32.

Helmings. — The race to which Queen Wealhtheow belonged. — 10 63.

Heming. — A kinsman of Garmund, perhaps nephew. — 28 54; 28 70.

Hengest. — A Danish leader. Takes command on the fall of Hnæf. — 17 33; 17 41.

Herebeald. — Eldest son of Hrethel, the Geatish king, and brother of Higelac. Killed by his younger brother Hæthcyn. — 34 43; 34 47.

Heremod. — A Danish king of a dynasty before the Scylding line. Was a source of great sorrow to his people. — 14 64; 25 59.

Hereric. — Referred to as uncle of Heardred, but otherwise unknown. — 31 60.

Hetwars. — Another name for the Franks. — 33 51.

Healfdene. — Grandson of Scyld and father of Hrothgar. Ruled the Danes long and well. — 2 5; 4 1; 8 14.

Heardred. — Son of Higelac and Hygd, king and queen of the Geats. Succeeds his father, with Beowulf as regent. Is slain by the sons of Ohthere. — 31 56; 33 63; 33 75.

Heathobards. — Race of Lombards, of which Froda is king. After Froda falls in battle with the Danes, Ingeld, his son, marries Hrothgar's daughter, Freaware, in order to heal the feud. — 30 1; 30 6.

Heatholaf. — A Wylfing warrior slain by Beowulf's father. — 8 5.

Heathoremes. — The people on whose shores Breca is cast by the waves during his contest with Beowulf. — 9 21.

Heorogar. — Elder brother of Hrothgar, and surnamed 'Weoroda Ræswa,' Prince of the Troopers. — 2 9; 8 12.

Hereward. — Son of the above. — 31 17.

Heort, Heorot. — The great mead-hall which King Hrothgar builds. It is invaded by Grendel for twelve years. Finally cleansed by Beowulf, the Geat. It is called Heort on account of the hart-antlers which decorate it. — 2 25; 3 32; 3 52.

Hildeburg. — Wife of Finn, daughter of Hoce, and related to Hnæf, — probably his sister. — 17 21; 18 34.

Hnæf. — Leader of a branch of the Danes called Half-Danes. Killed in the struggle at Finn's castle. — 17 19; 17 61.

Hondscio. — One of Beowulf's companions. Killed by Grendel just before Beowulf grappled with that monster. — 30 43.

Hoce. — Father of Hildeburg and probably of Hnæf. — 17 26.

Hrethel. — King of the Geats, father of Higelac, and grandfather of Beowulf. — 7 4; 34 39.

Hrethla. — Once used for Hrethel. — 7 82.

Hrethmen. — Another name for the Danes. — 7 73.

Hrethric. — Son of Hrothgar. — 18 65; 27 19.

Hreosna-beorh. — A promontory in Geat-land, near which Ohthere's sons made plundering raids. — 35 18.

Hrothgar. — The Danish king who built the hall Heort, but was long unable to enjoy it on account of Grendel's persecutions. Marries Wealhtheow, a Helming lady. Has two sons and a daughter. Is a typical Teutonic king, lavish of gifts. A devoted liegelord, as his lamentations over slain liegemen prove. Also very appreciative of kindness, as is shown by his loving gratitude to Beowulf. — 2 9; 2 12; 4 1; 8 10; 15 1; etc., etc.

Hrothmund. — Son of Hrothgar. — 18 65.

Hrothulf. — Probably a son of Halga, younger brother of Hrothgar. Certainly on terms of close intimacy in Hrothgar's palace. — 16 26; 18 57.

Hrunting. — Unferth's sword, lent to Beowulf. — 22 71; 25 9.

Hugs. — A race in alliance with the Franks and Frisians at the time of Higelac's fall. — 35 41.

Hun. — A Frisian warrior, probably general of the Hetwars. Gives Hengest a beautiful sword. — 18 19.

Hunferth. — Sometimes used for Unferth.

Hygelac, Higelac. — King of the Geats, uncle and liegelord of Beowulf, the hero of the poem. — His second wife is the lovely Hygd, daughter of Hæreth. The son of their union is Heardred. Is slain in a war with the Hugs, Franks, and Frisians combined. Beowulf is regent, and afterwards king of the Geats. — 4 6; 5 4; 28 34; 29 9; 29 21; 31 56.

Hygd. — Wife of Higelac, and daughter of Hæreth. There are some indications that she married Beowulf after she became a widow. — 28 37.

Ingeld. — Son of the Heathobard king, Froda. Marries Hrothgar's daughter, Freaware, in order to reconcile the two peoples. — 29 62; 30 32.

Ingwins. — Another name for the Danes. — 16 52; 20 69.

Jutes. — Name sometimes applied to Finn's people. — 17 22; 17 38; 18 17.

Lafing. — Name of a famous sword presented to Hengest by Hun. — 18 19.

Merewing. — A Frankish king, probably engaged in the war in which Higelac was slain. — 40 29.

Nægling. — Beowulf's sword. — 36 76.

Offa. — King of the Angles, and son of Garmund. Marries the terrible Thrytho who is so strongly contrasted with Hygd. — 28 59; 28 66.

Ohthere. — Son of Ongentheow, king of the Swedes. He is father of Eanmund and Eadgils. — 40 35; 40 39.

Onela. — Brother of Ohthere. — 36 15; 40 39.

Ongentheow. — King of Sweden, of the Scylfing dynasty. Married, perhaps, Elan, daughter of Healfdene. — 35 26; 41 16.

Oslaf. — A Dane of Hnæf's party. — 18 24.

Ravenswood. — The forest near which Hæthcyn was slain. — 40 31; 40 41.

Scefing. — Applied (1 4) to Scyld, and meaning 'son of Scef.'

Scyld. — Founder of the dynasty to which Hrothgar, his father, and grandfather belonged. He dies, and his body is put on a vessel, and set adrift. He goes from Daneland just as he had come to it — in a bark. — 1 4; 1 19; 1 27.

Scyldings. — The descendants of Scyld. They are also called Honor-Scyldings, Victory-Scyldings, War-Scyldings, etc. (See 'Danes,' above.) — 2 1; 7 1; 8 1.

Scylfings. — A Swedish royal line to which Wiglaf belonged. — 36 2.

Sigemund. — Son of Wæls, and uncle and father of Fitela. His struggle with a dragon is related in connection with Beowulf's deeds of prowess. — 14 38; 14 47.

Swerting. — Grandfather of Higelac, and father of Hrethel. — 19 11.

Swedes. — People of Sweden, ruled by the Scylfings. — 35 13.

Thrytho. — Wife of Offa, king of the Angles. Known for her fierce and unwomanly disposition. She is introduced as a contrast to the gentle Hygd, queen of Higelac. — 28 42; 28 56.

Unferth. — Son of Ecglaf, and seemingly a confidential courtier of Hrothgar. Taunts Beowulf for having taken part in the swimming-match. Lends Beowulf his sword when he goes to look for Grendel's mother. In the MS. sometimes written *Hunferth*. — 9 1; 18 41.

Wæls. — Father of Sigemund. — 14 60.

Wægmunding. — A name occasionally applied to Wiglaf and Beowulf, and perhaps derived from a common ancestor, Wægmund. — 36 6; 38 61.

Weders. — Another name for Geats or Wedergeats.

Wayland. — A fabulous smith mentioned in this poem and in other old Teutonic literature. — 7 83.

Wendels. — The people of Wulfgar, Hrothgar's messenger and retainer. (Perhaps = Vandals.) — 6 30.

Wealhtheow. — Wife of Hrothgar. Her queenly courtesy is well shown in the poem. — 10 55.

Weohstan, or Wihstan. — A Wægmunding, and father of Wiglaf. — 36 1.

Whale's Ness. — A prominent promontory, on which Beowulf's mound was built. — 38 52; 42 76.

Wiglaf. — Son of Wihstan, and related to Beowulf. He remains faithful to Beowulf in the fatal struggle with the fire-drake. Would rather die than leave his lord in his dire emergency. — 36 1; 36 3; 36 28.

Wonred. — Father of Wulf and Eofor. — 41 20; 41 26.

Wulf. — Son of Wonred. Engaged in the battle between Higelac's and Ongentheow's forces, and had a hand-to-hand fight with Ongentheow himself. Ongentheow disables him, and is thereupon slain by Eofor. — 41 19; 41 20.

Wulfgar. — Lord of the Wendels, and retainer of Hrothgar. — 6 18; 6 30.

Wylfings. — A people to whom belonged Heatholaf, who was slain by Ecgtheow. — 8 6; 8 16.

Yrmenlaf. — Younger brother of Æschere, the hero whose death grieved Hrothgar so deeply. — 21 4.

LIST OF WORDS AND PHRASES

NOT IN GENERAL USE.

ATHELING. — Prince, nobleman.

BAIRN. — Son, child.

BARROW. — Mound, rounded hill, funeral-mound.

BATTLE-SARK. — Armor.

BEAKER. — Cup, drinking-vessel.

BEGEAR. — Prepare.

BIGHT. — Bay, sea.

BILL. — Sword.

BOSS. — Ornamental projection.

BRACTEATE. — A round ornament on a necklace.

BRAND. — Sword.

BURN. — Stream.

BURNIE. — Armor.

CARLE. — Man, hero.

EARL. — Nobleman, any brave man.

EKE. — Also.

EMPRISE. — Enterprise, undertaking.

ERST. — Formerly.

ERST-WORTHY. — Worthy for a long time past.

FAIN. — Glad.

FERRY. — Bear, carry.

FEY. — Fated, doomed.

FLOAT. — Vessel, ship.

FOIN. — To lunge (Shaks.).

GLORY OF KINGS. — God.

GREWSOME. — Cruel, fierce.

HEFT. — Handle, hilt; used by synecdoche for 'sword.'

HELM. — Helmet, protector.

HENCHMAN. — Retainer, vassal.

HIGHT. — Am (was) named.

HOLM. — Ocean, curved surface of the sea.

HIMSEEMED. — (It) seemed to him.

LIEF. — Dear, valued.

MERE. — Sea; in compounds, 'mere-ways,' ' mere-currents,' etc.

MICKLE. — Much.

NATHLESS. — Nevertheless.

NAZE. — Edge (nose).

NESS. — Edge.

NICKER. — Sea-beast.

QUIT, QUITE. — Requite.

RATHE. — Quickly.

REAVE. — Bereave, deprive.

SAIL-ROAD. — Sea.

SETTLE. — Seat, bench.

SKINKER. — One who pours.

SOOTHLY. — Truly.

SWINGE. — Stroke, blow.

TARGE, TARGET. — Shield.

THROUGHLY. — Thoroughly.

TOLD. — Counted.

UNCANNY. — Ill-featured, grizzly.

UNNETHE. — Difficult.

WAR-SPEED. — Success in war.

WEB. — Tapestry (that which is 'woven ').

WEEDED. — Clad (cf. widow's weeds).

WEEN. — Suppose, imagine.

WEIRD. — Fate, Providence.

WHILOM. — At times, formerly, often.

WIELDER. — Ruler. Often used of God; also in compounds, as ' Wielder of Glory,' ' Wielder of Worship.'

WIGHT. — Creature.

WOLD. — Plain, extended surface.

WOT. — Knows.

YOUNKER. — Youth.

BEOWULF.

I.

THE LIFE AND DEATH OF SCYLD.

Lo ! the Spear-Danes' glory through splendid achievements
The folk-kings' former fame we have heard of,
How princes displayed then their prowess-in-battle.
Oft Scyld the Scefing from scathers in numbers
5 From many a people their mead-benches tore.
Since first he found him friendless and ·wretched,
The earl had had terror : comfort he got for it,
Waked 'neath the welkin, world-honor gained,
Till all his neighbors o'er sea were compelled to
10 Bow to his bidding and bring him their tribute :
An excellent atheling !   After was borne him
A son and heir, young in his dwelling,
Whom God-Father sent to solace the people.
He had marked the misery malice had caused them,
15 [1] That reaved of their rulers they wretched had erstwhile [2]
Long been afflicted.   The Lord, in requital,
Wielder of Glory, with world-honor blessed him.
Famed was Beowulf, far spread the glory
Of Scyld's great son in the lands of the Danemen.

The famous race of Spear-Danes.

Scyld, their mighty king, in honor of whom they are often called Scyld-ings. He is the great-grandfather of Hrothgar, so prominent in the poem.

A son is born to him, who receives the name of Beowulf — a name afterwards made so famous by the hero of the poem.

---

[1] For the 'þæt' of verse 15, Sievers suggests 'þá' (= which).   If this be accepted, the sentence 'He had . . . afflicted' will read : *He (i.e.* God) *had perceived the malice-caused sorrow which they, lordless, had formerly long endured.*

[2] For 'aldor-léase' (15) Gr. suggested 'aldor-ceare': *He perceived their distress, that they formerly had suffered life-sorrow a long while.*

The ideal Teutonic king lavishes gifts on his vassals.

20 So the carle that is young, by kindnesses rendered
The friends of his father, with fees in abundance
Must be able to earn that when age approacheth
Eager companions aid him requitingly,
When war assaults him serve him as liegemen :
25 By praise-worthy actions must honor be got
'Mong all of the races.   At the hour that was fated

Scyld dies at the hour appointed by Fate.

Scyld then departed to the All-Father's keeping
Warlike to wend him ; away then they bare him
To the flood of the current, his fond-loving comrades,
30 As himself he had bidden, while the friend of the Scyldings
Word-sway wielded, and the well-lovèd land-prince
Long did rule them.[1]   The ring-stemmèd vessel,
Bark of the athelīng, lay there at anchor,
Icy in glimmer and eager for sailing ;

By his own request, his body is laid on a vessel and wafted seaward.

35 The belovèd leader laid they down there,
Giver of rings, on the breast of the vessel,
The famed by the mainmast.   A many of jewels,
Of fretted embossings, from far-lands brought over,
Was placed near at hand then ; and heard I not ever
40 That a folk ever furnished a float more superbly
With weapons of warfare, weeds for the battle,
Bills and burnies ; on his bosom sparkled
Many a jewel that with him must travel
On the flush of the flood afar on the current.
45 And favors no fewer they furnished him soothly,
Excellent folk-gems, than others had given him

He leaves Dane-land on the breast of a bark.

Who when first he was born outward did send him
Lone on the main, the merest of infants :
And a gold-fashioned standard they stretched under heaven

---

[1] A very difficult passage.   'Āhte' (31) has no object.   H. supplies 'ge-weald' from the context; and our translation is based upon this assumption, though it is far from satisfactory.   Kl. suggests 'lændagas' for 'lange': *And the beloved land-prince enjoyed (had) his transitory days (i.e. lived).*   B. sug-gests a dislocation; but this is a dangerous doctrine, pushed rather far by that eminent scholar.

50 High o'er his head, let the holm-currents bear him,
   Seaward consigned him : sad was their spirit,
   Their mood very mournful.   Men are not able
   Soothly to tell us, they in halls who reside,[1]
   Heroes under heaven, to what haven he hied.

No one knows
whither the boat
drifted.

II.

SCYLD'S SUCCESSORS. — HROTHGAR'S GREAT MEAD-HALL.

In the boroughs then Beowulf, bairn of the Scyldings,
Belovèd land-prince, for long-lasting season
Was famed mid the folk (his father departed,
The prince from his dwelling), till afterward sprang

Beowulf succeeds
his father Scyld.

5 Great-minded Healfdene; the Danes in his lifetime
   He graciously governed, grim-mooded, agèd.

Healfdene's birth.

   Four bairns of his body born in succession
   Woke in the world, war-troopers' leader
   Heorogar, Hrothgar, and Halga the good ;
10 Heard I that Elan was Ongentheow's consort,
   The well-beloved bedmate of the War-Scylfing leader.

He has three sons
— one of them,
Hrothgar — and a
daughter named
Elan. Hrothgar
becomes a mighty
king.

   Then glory in battle to Hrothgar was given,
   Waxing of war-fame, that willingly kinsmen
   Obeyed his bidding, till the boys grew to manhood,
15 A numerous band.   It burned in his spirit
   To urge his folk to found a great building,
   A mead-hall grander than men of the era

He is eager to
build a great hall
in which he may
feast his retainers.

   Ever had heard of, and in it to share
   With young and old all of the blessings
20 The Lord had allowed him, save life and retainers.
   Then the work I find afar was assigned

[1] The reading of the H.-So. text has been quite closely followed; but some
eminent scholars read 'séle-rædenne' for 'sele-rædende.' If that be adopted,
the passage will read: *Men cannot tell us, indeed, the order of Fate, etc.*
'Sele-rædende' has two things to support it: (1) v. 1347; (2) it affords a
parallel to 'men' in v. 50.

To many races in middle-earth's regions,
To adorn the great folk-hall. In due time it happened
Early 'mong men, that 'twas finished entirely,

The hall is completed, and is called Heort, or Heorot.

25 The greatest of hall-buildings ; Heorot he named it
Who wide-reaching word-sway wielded 'mong earlmen.
His promise he brake not, rings he lavished,
Treasure at banquet.   Towered the hall up
High and horn-crested, huge between antlers :

30 It battle-waves bided, the blasting fire-demon ;
Ere long then from hottest hatred must sword-wrath
Arise for a woman's husband and father.

The monster Grendel is madly envious of the Danemen's joy.

Then the mighty war-spirit[1] endured for a season,
Bore it bitterly, he who bided in darkness,

35 That light-hearted laughter loud in the building
Greeted him daily ; there was dulcet harp-music,
Clear song of the singer.   He said that was able

[The course of the story is interrupted by a short reference to some old account of the creation.]

To tell from of old earthmen's beginnings,
That Father Almighty earth had created,

40 The winsome wold that the water encircleth,
Set exultingly the sun's and the moon's beams
To lavish their lustre on land-folk and races,
And earth He embellished in all her regions
With limbs and leaves ; life He bestowed too

45 On all the kindreds that live under heaven.

The glee of the warriors is overcast by a horrible dread.

So blessed with abundance, brimming with joyance,
The warriors abided, till a certain one gan to
Dog them with deeds of direfullest malice,
A foe in the hall-building : this horrible stranger[2]

50 Was Grendel entitled, the march-stepper famous
Who[3] dwelt in the moor-fens, the marsh and the fastness ;
The wan-mooded being abode for a season

---

[1] R. and t. B. prefer ' ellor-gæst ' to ' ellen-gæst ' (86) : *Then the stranger from afar endured, etc.*

[2] Some authorities would translate ' *demon* ' instead of ' *stranger.* '

[3] Some authorities arrange differently, and render : *Who dwelt in the moor-fens, the marsh and the fastness, the land of the giant-race.*

In the land of the giants, when the Lord and Creator
Had banned him and branded. For that bitter murder,
55 The killing of Abel, all-ruling Father
The kindred of Cain crushed with His vengeance ;
In the feud He rejoiced not, but far away drove him
From kindred and kind, that crime to atone for,
Meter of Justice. Thence ill-favored creatures,
60 Elves and giants, monsters of ocean,
Came into being, and the giants that longtime
Grappled with God ; He gave them requital.

Cain is referred to as a progenitor of Grendel, and of monsters in general.

III.

GRENDEL THE MURDERER.

When the sun was sunken, he set out to visit
The lofty hall-building, how the Ring-Danes had used it
For beds and benches when the banquet was over.
Then he found there reposing many a noble
5 Asleep after supper ; sorrow the heroes,[1]
Misery knew not. The monster of evil
Greedy and cruel tarried but little,
Fell and frantic, and forced from their slumbers
Thirty of thanemen ; thence he departed
10 Leaping and laughing, his lair to return to,
With surfeit of slaughter sallying homeward.
In the dusk of the dawning, as the day was just breaking,
Was Grendel's prowess revealed to the warriors :
Then, his meal-taking finished, a moan was uplifted,
15 Morning-cry mighty. The man-ruler famous,
The long-worthy atheling, sat very woful,
Suffered great sorrow, sighed for his liegemen,

Grendel attacks the sleeping heroes.

He drags off thirty of them, and devours them.

A cry of agony goes up when Grendel's horrible deed is fully realized.

[1] The translation is based on 'weras,' adopted by H.-So. — K. and Th.
read 'wera' and, arranging differently, render 119(2)-120: *They knew not
sorrow, the wretchedness of man, aught of misfortune.* — For 'unhælo' (120)
R. suggests 'unfælo.': *The uncanny creature, greedy and cruel, etc.*

. When they had seen the track of the hateful pursuer,
The spirit accursèd : too crushing that sorrow,

The monster re-
turns the next
night.

20 Too loathsome and lasting.   Not longer he tarried,
But one night after continued his slaughter
Shameless and shocking, shrinking but little
From malice and murder ; they mastered him fully.
He was easy to find then who otherwhere looked for
25 A pleasanter place of repose in the lodges,
A bed in the bowers.   Then was brought to his notice
Told him truly by token apparent
The hall-thane's hatred : he held himself after
Further and faster who the foeman did baffle.
30 [1] So ruled he and strongly strove against justice
Lone against all men, till empty uptowered

King Hrothgar's
agony and sus-
pense last twelve
years.

The choicest of houses.   Long was the season :
Twelve-winters' time torture suffered
The friend of the Scyldings, every affliction,
35 Endless agony ; hence it after [2] became
Certainly known to the children of men
Sadly in measures, that long against Hrothgar
Grendel struggled : — his grudges he cherished,
Murderous malice, many a winter,
40 Strife unremitting, and peacefully wished he
[3] Life-woe to lift from no liegeman at all of
The men of the Dane-folk, for money to settle,
No counsellor needed count for a moment

---

[1] S. rearranges and translates : *So he ruled and struggled unjustly, one against all, till the noblest of buildings stood useless (it was a long while) twelve years' time : the friend of the Scyldings suffered distress, every woe, great sorrows,* etc.

[2] For 'syðÐan,' B. suggests 'sárewidum' : *Hence in mournful words it became well known,* etc.   Various other words beginning with 's' have been conjectured.

[3] The H.-So. glossary is very inconsistent in referring to this passage. — 'Sibbe' (154), which H.-So. regards as an instr., B. takes as accus., obj. of 'wolde.'   Putting a comma after Deniga, he renders : *He did not desire peace with any of the Danes, nor did he wish to remove their life-woe, nor to settle for money.*

On handsome amends at the hands of the murderer ;
45 The monster of evil fiercely did harass,
The ill-planning death-shade, both elder and younger,
Trapping and tricking them.   He trod every night then
The mist-covered moor-fens ; men do not know where
Witches and wizards wander and ramble.
50 So the foe of mankind many of evils
Grievous injuries, often accomplished,
Horrible hermit ; Heort he frequented,
Gem-bedecked palace, when night-shades had fallen
(Since God did oppose him, not the throne could he touch,[1]
55 The light-flashing jewel, love of Him knew not).
'Twas a fearful affliction to the friend of the Scyldings
Soul-crushing sorrow.   Not seldom in private
Sat the king in his council ; conference held they
What the braves should determine 'gainst terrors unlooked for.
60 At the shrines of their idols often they promised
Gifts and offerings, earnestly prayed they
The devil from hell would help them to lighten
Their people's oppression.   Such practice they used then,
Hope of the heathen ; hell they remembered
65 In innermost spirit, God they knew not,
Judge of their actions, All-wielding Ruler,
No praise could they give the Guardian of Heaven,
The Wielder of Glory.   Woe will be his who
Through furious hatred his spirit shall drive to
70 The clutch of the fire, no comfort shall look for,
Wax no wiser ; well for the man who,
Living his life-days, his Lord may face
And find defence in his Father's embrace !

Grendel is unremitting in his persecutions.

God is against the monster.

The king and his council deliberate in vain.

They invoke the aid of their gods.

The true God they do not know.

---

[1] Of this difficult passage the following interpretations among others are given : (1) Though Grendel has frequented Heorot as a demon, he could not become ruler of the Danes, on account of his hostility to God. (2) Hrothgar was much grieved that Grendel had not appeared before his throne to receive presents. (3) He was not permitted to devastate the hall, on account of the Creator ; *i.e.* God wished to make his visit fatal to him. — Ne . . . wisse (169) W. renders : *Nor had he any desire to do so ;* ' his ' being obj. gen. = danach.

IV.

BEOWULF GOES TO HROTHGAR'S ASSISTANCE.

Hrothgar sees no
way of escape from
the persecutions of
Grendel.

So Healfdene's kinsman constantly mused on
His long-lasting sorrow; the battle-thane clever
Was not anywise able evils to 'scape from:
Too crushing the sorrow that came to the people,
5 Loathsome and lasting the life-grinding torture,

Beowulf, the Geat,
hero of the poem,
hears of Hrothgar's
sorrow, and re-
solves to go to his
assistance.

Greatest of night-woes. So Higelac's liegeman,
Good amid Geatmen, of Grendel's achievements
Heard in his home:[1] of heroes then living
He was stoutest and strongest, sturdy and noble.
10 He bade them prepare him a bark that was trusty;
He said he the war-king would seek o'er the ocean,
The folk-leader noble, since he needed retainers.
For the perilous project prudent companions
Chided him little, though loving him dearly;
15 They egged the brave atheling, augured him glory.

With fourteen care-
fully chosen com-
panions, he sets out
for Dane-land.

The excellent knight from the folk of the Geatmen
Had liegemen selected, likest to prove them
Trustworthy warriors; with fourteen companions
The vessel he looked for; a liegeman then showed them,
20 A sea-crafty man, the bounds of the country.
Fast the days fleeted; the float was a-water,
The craft by the cliff. Clomb to the prow then
Well-equipped warriors: the wave-currents twisted
The sea on the sand; soldiers then carried
25 On the breast of the vessel bright-shining jewels,
Handsome war-armor; heroes outshoved then,
Warmen the wood-ship, on its wished-for adventure.

---

[1] 'From hám' (194) is much disputed. One rendering is: *Beowulf, being
away from home, heard of Hrothgar's troubles, etc.* Another, that adopted by
S. and endorsed in the H.-So. notes, is: *B. heard from his neighborhood (neighbors),* i.e. *in his home, etc.* A third is: *B., being at home, heard this as
occurring away from home.* The H.-So. glossary and notes conflict.

The foamy-necked floater fanned by the breeze,
Likest a bird, glided the waters,

The vessel sails
like a bird.

30 'Till twenty and four hours thereafter
The twist-stemmèd vessel had traveled such distance
That the sailing-men saw the sloping embankments,
The sea-cliffs gleaming, precipitous mountains,
Nesses enormous : they were nearing the limits

In twenty-four
hours they reach
the shores of
Hrothgar's domin-
ions.

35 At the end of the ocean.[1] Up thence quickly
The men of the Weders clomb to the mainland,
Fastened their vessel (battle-weeds rattled,
War-burnies clattered) ; the Wielder they thanked
That the ways o'er the waters had waxen so gentle.

40 Then well from the cliff-edge the guard of the Scyldings
Who the sea-cliffs should see to, saw o'er the gangway
Brave ones bearing beauteous targets,
Armor all ready ; anxiously thought he,
Musing and wondering what men were approaching.

They are hailed by
the Danish coast-
guard.

45 High on his horse then Hrothgar's retainer
Turned him to coastward, mightily brandished
His lance in his hands, questioned with boldness :
"Who are ye men here, mail-covered warriors
Clad in your corslets, come thus a-driving

His challenge.

50 A high-riding ship o'er the shoals of the waters,
[2] And hither 'neath helmets have hied o'er the ocean?

---

[1] 'Eoletes' (224) is marked with a (?) by H.-So.: our rendering simply
follows his conjecture. — Other conjectures as to 'eolet' are: (1) *voyage ;*
(2) *toil, labor ;* (3) *hasty journey.*

[2] The lacuna of the MS. at this point has been supplied by various conjectures. The reading adopted by H.So. has been rendered in the above translation.
W., like H.-So. makes 'ic' the beginning of a new sentence ; but, for 'helmas
bæron,' he reads 'hringed-stefnan.' This has the advantage of giving a
parallel to 'brontne céol' instead of a kenning for 'go.' — B. puts the (?)
after 'holmas,' and begins a new sentence at the middle of the line. Translate : *What warriors are ye, clad in armor, who have thus come bringing the
foaming vessel over the water-way, hither over the seas? For some time on
the wall I have been coast-guard, etc.* S. endorses most of what B. says, but
leaves out 'on the wall' in the last sentence. If W.'s 'hringed-stefnan' be
accepted, change line 51 above to, *A ring-stemmed vessel hither o'ersea?*

I have been strand-guard, standing as warden,
Lest enemies ever anywise ravage
Danish dominions with army of war-ships.
55 More boldly never have warriors ventured
Hither to come ; of kinsmen's approval,
Word-leave of warriors, I ween that ye surely

Nothing have known.   Never a greater one
Of earls o'er the earth have *I* had a sight of
60 Than is one of your number, a hero in armor ;
No low-ranking fellow [1] adorned with his weapons,
But launching them little, unless looks are deceiving,
And striking appearance.   Ere ye pass on your journey
As treacherous spies to the land of the Scyldings
65 And farther fare, I fully must know now
What race ye belong to.   Ye far-away dwellers,
Sea-faring sailors, my simple opinion
Hear ye and hearken : haste is most fitting
Plainly to tell me what place ye are come from.''

V.

THE GEATS REACH HEOROT.

The chief of the strangers rendered him answer,
War-troopers' leader, and word-treasure opened :

'' We are sprung from the lineage of the people of Geatland,
And Higelac's hearth-friends.   To heroes unnumbered

5 My father was known, a noble head-warrior
Ecgtheow titled ; many a winter
He lived with the people, ere he passed on his journey,
Old from his dwelling ; each of the counsellors
Widely mid world-folk well remembers him.

10 We, kindly of spirit, the lord of thy people,
The son of King Healfdene, have come here to visit,

---

[1] ' Seld-guma ' (249) is variously rendered : (1) *housecarle ;* (2) *home-stayer ;*
(3) *common man.* Dr. H. Wood suggests *a man-at-arms in another's house.*

Folk-troop's defender: be free in thy counsels!
To the noble one bear we a weighty commission,
The helm of the Danemen; we shall hide, I ween,
15 Naught of our message. Thou know'st if it happen,
As we soothly heard say, that some savage despoiler,
Some hidden pursuer, on nights that are murky
By deeds very direful 'mid the Danemen exhibits
Hatred unheard of, horrid destruction
20 And the falling of dead. From feelings least selfish
I am able to render counsel to Hrothgar,
How he, wise and worthy, may worst the destroyer,
If the anguish of sorrow should ever be lessened,[1]
Comfort come to him, and care-waves grow cooler,
25 Or ever hereafter he agony suffer
And troublous distress, while towereth upward
The handsomest of houses high on the summit."
Bestriding his stallion, the strand-watchman answered,
The doughty retainer: " The difference surely
30 'Twixt words and works, the warlike shield-bearer
Who judgeth wisely well shall determine.
This band, I hear, beareth no malice
To the prince of the Scyldings. Pass ye then onward
With weapons and armor. I shall lead you in person;
35 To my war-trusty vassals command I shall issue
To keep from all injury your excellent vessel,
Your fresh-tarred craft, 'gainst every opposer
Close by the sea-shore, till the curvèd-neckèd bark shall
Waft back again the well-beloved hero
40 O'er the way of the water to Weder dominions.
To warrior so great 'twill be granted sure
In the storm of strife to stand secure."
Onward they fared then (the vessel lay quiet,
The broad-bosomed bark was bound by its cable,

Is it true that a monster is slaying Danish heroes?

I can help your king to free himself from this horrible creature.

The coast-guard reminds Beowulf that it is easier to say than to do.

I am satisfied of your good intentions, and shall lead you to the palace.

Your boat shall be well cared for during your stay here.

He again compliments Beowulf.

---

[1] 'Edwendan' (280) B. takes to be the subs. 'edwenden' (cf. 1775); and
'bisigu' he takes as gen. sing., limiting 'edwenden': *If reparation for sorrows is ever to come.* This is supported by t. B.

45 Firmly at anchor) ; the boar-signs glistened [1]
   Bright on the visors vivid with gilding,
   Blaze-hardened, brilliant ; the boar acted warden.
   The heroes hastened, hurried the liegemen,

The land is per-   Descended together, till they saw the great palace,
haps rolling.
50 The well-fashioned wassail-hall wondrous and gleaming :

Heorot flashes on   'Mid world-folk and kindreds that was widest reputed
their view.
   Of halls under heaven which the hero abode in ;
   Its lustre enlightened lands without number.
   Then the battle-brave hero showed them the glittering

55 Court of the bold ones, that they easily thither
   Might fare on their journey ; the aforementioned warrior
   Turning his courser, quoth as he left them :

The coast-guard,   " 'Tis time I were faring ; Father Almighty
having discharged
his duty, bids them   Grant you His grace, and give you to journey
God-speed.
60 Safe on your mission !   To the sea I will get me
   'Gainst hostile warriors as warden to stand."

VI.

BEOWULF INTRODUCES HIMSELF AT THE PALACE.

   The highway glistened with many-hued pebble,
   A by-path led the liegemen together.
   [2] Firm and hand-locked the war-burnie glistened,
   The ring-sword radiant rang 'mid the armor

5 As the party was approaching the palace together
They set their   In warlike equipments.   'Gainst the wall of the building
arms and armor
against the wall.   Their wide-fashioned war-shields they weary did set then,

---

[1] Combining the emendations of B. and t. B., we may read: *The boar-
images glistened . . . brilliant, protected the life of the war-mooded man.*   They
read ' ferh-wearde ' (305) and ' gúðmódgum men ' (306).

[2] Instead of the punctuation given by H.-So., S. proposed to insert a comma
after ' scír ' (322), and to take ' hring-íren ' as meaning ' ring-mail ' and as
parallel with ' gúð-byrne.'   The passage would then read: *The firm and
hand-locked war-burnie shone, bright ring-mail, rang 'mid the armor, etc.*

Battle-shields sturdy; benchward they turned then;
Their battle-sarks rattled, the gear of the heroes;
10 The lances stood up then, all in a cluster,
The arms of the seamen, ashen-shafts mounted
With edges of iron: the armor-clad troopers
Were decked with weapons. Then a proud-mooded hero

A Danish hero asks them whence and why they are come.

Asked of the champions questions of lineage:
15 " From what borders bear ye your battle-shields plated,
Gilded and gleaming, your gray-colored burnies,
Helmets with visors and heap of war-lances? —
To Hrothgar the king I am servant and liegeman.
'Mong folk from far-lands found I have never
20 Men so many of mien more courageous.,

He expresses no little admiration for the strangers.

I ween that from valor, nowise as outlaws,
But from greatness of soul ye sought for King Hrothgar."
Then the strength-famous earlman answer rendered,

Beowulf replies.

The proud-mooded Wederchief replied to his question,
25 Hardy 'neath helmet: " Higelac's mates are we;
Beowulf hight I. To the bairn of Healfdene,

We are Higelac's table-companions, and bear an important commission to your prince.

The famous folk-leader, I freely will tell
To thy prince my commission, if pleasantly hearing
He'll grant we may greet him so gracious to all men."
30 Wulfgar replied then (he was prince of the Wendels,
His boldness of spirit was known unto many,
His prowess and prudence): " The prince of the Scyldings,
The friend-lord of Danemen, I will ask of thy journey,

Wulfgar, the thane, says that he will go and ask Hrothgar whether he will see the strangers.

The giver of rings, as thou urgest me do it,
35 The folk-chief famous, and inform thee early
What answer the good one mindeth to render me."
He turned then hurriedly where Hrothgar was sitting,
¹ Old and hoary, his earlmen attending him;
The strength-famous went till he stood at the shoulder
40 Of the lord of the Danemen, of courteous thanemen
The custom he minded. Wulfgar addressed then
His friendly liegelord: " Folk of the Geatmen

¹ Gr. and others translate 'unhár' by 'bald': *old and bald.*

He thereupon
urges his liegelord
to receive the visit-
ors courteously.   45

O'er the way of the waters are wafted hither,
Faring from far-lands : the foremost in rank
The battle-champions Beowulf title.
They make this petition : with thee, O my chieftain,
To be granted a conference ; O gracious King Hrothgar,
Friendly answer refuse not to give them !

Hrothgar, too, is
struck with Beo-
wulf's appearance. 50

In war-trappings weeded worthy they seem
Of earls to be honored ; sure the atheling is doughty
Who headed the heroes hitherward coming."

VII.

HROTHGAR AND BEOWULF.

Hrothgar remem-
bers Beowulf as a
youth, and also
remembers his
father.

Hrothgar answered, helm of the Scyldings :
" I remember this man as the merest of striplings.
His father long dead now was Ecgtheow titled,
Him Hrethel the Geatman granted at home his

5 One only daughter ; his battle-brave son
Is come but now, sought a trustworthy friend.
Seafaring sailors asserted it then,

Beowulf is re-
ported to have the
strength of thirty
men.

Who valuable gift-gems of the Geatmen[1] carried
As peace-offering thither, that he thirty men's grapple

God hath sent him
to our rescue.

10 Has in his hand, the hero-in-battle.
The holy Creator usward sent him,
To West-Dane warriors, I ween, for to render
'Gainst Grendel's grimness gracious assistance :
I shall give to the good one gift-gems for courage.

15 Hasten to bid them hither to speed them,[2]
To see assembled this circle of kinsmen ;
Tell them expressly they're welcome in sooth to
The men of the Danes."   To the door of the building

[1] Some render ' gif-sceattas ' by ' tribute.' — ' Géata ' B. and Th. emended to
' Géatum.' If this be accepted, change ' *of* the Geatmen ' to ' *to* the Geatmen.'
[2] If t. B.'s emendation of vv. 386, 387 be accepted, the two lines, ' Hasten
... kinsmen ' will read : *Hasten thou, bid the throng of kinsmen go into the
hall together.*

Wulfgar went then, this word-message shouted:

20 " My victorious liegelord bade me to tell you,
The East-Danes' atheling, that your origin knows he,
And o'er wave-billows wafted ye welcome are hither,
Valiant of spirit. Ye straightway may enter
Clad in corslets, cased in your helmets,
25 To see King Hrothgar. Here let your battle-boards,
Wood-spears and war-shafts, await your conferring."
The mighty one rose then, with many a liegeman,
An excellent thane-group; some there did await them,
And as bid of the brave one the battle-gear guarded.
30 Together they hied them, while the hero did guide them,
'Neath Heorot's roof; the high-minded went then
Sturdy 'neath helmet till he stood in the building.
Beowulf spake (his burnie did glisten,
His armor seamed over by the art of the craftsman) :

35 " Hail thou, Hrothgar ! I am Higelac's kinsman
And vassal forsooth ; many a wonder
I dared as a stripling. The doings of Grendel,
In far-off fatherland I fully did know of:
Sea-farers tell us, this hall-building standeth,
40 Excellent edifice, empty and useless
To all the earlmen after evenlight's glimmer
'Neath heaven's bright hues hath hidden its glory.
This my earls then urged me, the most excellent of them,
Carles very clever, to come and assist thee,
45 Folk-leader Hrothgar ; fully they knew of
The strength of my body. Themselves they beheld me

When I came from the contest, when covered with gore
Foes I escaped from, where five [1] I had bound,

---

[1] For 420 (*b*) and 421 (*a*), B. suggests: þær ic (on) fífelgeban ýðde
eotena cyn = *where I in the ocean destroyed the eoten-race.* — t. B. accepts B.'s
"brilliant" 'fífelgeban,' omits ' on,' emends ' cyn' to ' hám,' arranging: þær ic
fífelgeban ýðde, eotena hám = *where I desolated the ocean, the home of the
eotens.* — This would be better but for changing 'cyn' to 'hám.' — I suggest:
þær ic fífelgeband (*cf.* nhd. Bande) ýðde, eotena cyn = *where I conquered the
monster band, the race of the eotens.* This makes no change except to read
'fífel' for 'fífe.'

The giant-race wasted, in the waters destroying
50 The nickers by night, bore numberless sorrows,
The Weders avengèd (woes had they suffered)
Enemies ravaged ; alone now with Grendel

He intends to fight
Grendel unaided.

I shall manage the matter, with the monster of evil,
The giant, decide it.   Thee I would therefore
55 Beg of thy bounty, Bright-Danish chieftain,
Lord of the Scyldings, this single petition :
Not to refuse me, defender of warriors,
Friend-lord of folks, so far have I sought thee,
That *I* may unaided, my earlmen assisting me,
60 This brave-mooded war-band, purify Heorot.
I have heard on inquiry, the horrible creature

Since the monster
uses no weapons,

From veriest rashness recks not for weapons ;
I this do scorn then, so be Higelac gracious,
My liegelord belovèd, lenient of spirit,
65 To bear a blade or a broad-fashioned target,
A shield to the onset ; only with hand-grip

I, too, shall disdain
to use any.

The foe I must grapple, fight for my life then,
Foeman with foeman ; he fain must rely on
The doom of the Lord whom death layeth hold of.

Should he crush
me, he will eat my
companions as he
has eaten thy
thanes.

70 I ween he will wish, if he win in the struggle,
To eat in the war-hall earls of the Geat-folk,
Boldly to swallow[1] them, as of yore he did often
The best of the Hrethmen !   Thou needest not trouble
A head-watch to give me ;[2] he will have me dripping

---

[1] 'Unforhte' (444) is much disputed. — H.-So. wavers between adj. and adv. Gr. and B. take it as an adv. modifying *etan : Will eat the Geats fearlessly.* — Kl. considers this reading absurd, and proposes ' anforhte ' = timid. — Understanding ' unforhte ' as an adj. has this advantage, viz. that it gives a parallel to 'Geátena leóde ': but to take it as an adv. is more natural. Furthermore, to call the Geats ' brave ' might, at this point, seem like an implied thrust at the Danes, so long helpless; while to call his own men ' timid ' would be befouling his own nest.

[2] For 'head-watch,' *cf.* H.-So. notes and *cf.* v. 2910. — Th. translates: *Thou wilt not need my head to hide* (*i.e.*, thou wilt have no occasion to bury me, as Grendel will devour me whole). — Simrock imagines a kind of dead-watch. —

75 And dreary with gore, if death overtake me,[1]
Will bear me off bleeding, biting and mouthing me,
The hermit will eat me, heedless of pity,
Marking the moor-fens ; no more wilt thou need then
Find me my food.[2] If I fall in the battle,
80 Send to Higelac the armor that serveth
To shield my bosom, the best of equipments,
Richest of ring-mails ; 'tis the relic of Hrethla,
The work of Wayland.   Goes Weird as she must go ! ''

In case of my defeat, thou wilt not have the trouble of burying me.

Should I fall, send my armor to my lord, King Higelac.

Weird is supreme.

VIII.

HROTHGAR AND BEOWULF. — *Continued.*

Hrothgar discoursed, helm of the Scyldings :
'' To defend our folk and to furnish assistance,[3]
Thou soughtest us hither, good friend Beowulf.
The fiercest of feuds thy father engaged in,
5 Heatholaf killed he in hand-to-hand conflict
'Mid Wilfingish warriors ; then the Wederish people
For fear of a feud were forced to disown him.
Thence flying he fled to the folk of the South-Danes,

Hrothgar responds.

Reminiscences of Beowulf's father, Ecgtheow.

Dr. H. Wood suggests: *Thou wilt not have to bury so much as my head* (for Grendel will be a thorough undertaker), — grim humor.

[1] S. proposes a colon after 'nimeð' (l. 447). This would make no essential change in the translation.

[2] Owing to the vagueness of 'feorme' (451), this passage is variously translated. In our translation, H.-So.'s glossary has been quite closely followed. This agrees substantially with B.'s translation (P. and B. XII. 87). R. translates: *Thou needst not take care longer as to the consumption of my dead body.* 'Líc' is also a crux here, as it may mean living body or dead body.

[3] B. and S. reject the reading given in H.-So., and suggested by Grtvg. B. suggests for 457–458 :

> wáere-ryhtum þú, wine mín Béowulf,
> and for ár-stafum úsic sóhtest.

This means : *From the obligations of clientage, my friend Beowulf, and for assistance thou hast sought us.* —This gives coherence to Hrothgar's opening remarks in VIII., and also introduces a new motive for Beowulf's coming to Hrothgar's aid.

The race of the Scyldings, o'er the roll of the waters ;
10 I had lately begun then to govern the Danemen,
The hoard-seat of heroes held in my youth,
Rich in its jewels : dead was Heregar,
My kinsman and elder had earth-joys forsaken,
Healfdene his bairn.   He was better than I am !
15 That feud thereafter for a fee I compounded ;
O'er the weltering waters to the Wilfings I sent
Ornaments old ; oaths did he swear me.

Hrothgar recounts
to Beowulf the
horrors of Grendel's
persecutions.

It pains me in spirit to any to tell it,
What grief in Heorot Grendel hath caused me,
20 What horror unlooked-for, by hatred unceasing.
Waned is my war-band, wasted my hall-troop ;
Weird hath offcast them to the clutches of Grendel.
God can easily hinder the scather
From deeds so direful.   Oft drunken with beer

My thanes have
made many boasts,
but have not exe-
cuted them.

25 O'er the ale-vessel promised warriors in armor
They would willingly wait on the wassailing-benches
A grapple with Grendel, with grimmest of edges.
Then this mead-hall at morning with murder was reeking,
The building was bloody at breaking of daylight,
30 The bench-deals all flooded, dripping and bloodied,
The folk-hall was gory : I had fewer retainers,
Dear-beloved warriors, whom death had laid hold of.

Sit down to the
feast, and give us
comfort.
A bench is made
ready for Beowulf
and his party.

Sit at the feast now, thy intents unto heroes,[1]
Thy victor-fame show, as thy spirit doth urge thee !"
35 For the men of the Geats then together assembled,
In the beer-hall blithesome a bench was made ready ;
There warlike in spirit they went to be seated,
Proud and exultant.   A liegeman did service,

---

[1] *Sit now at the feast, and disclose thy purposes to the victorious heroes, as thy spirit urges.* — Kl. reaches the above translation by erasing the comma after ' meoto' and reading ' sige-hréðsecgum.' — There are other and bolder emendations and suggestions. Of these the boldest is to regard ' meoto' as a verb (imperative), and read ' on sæl': *Think upon gayety, etc.* — All the renderings are unsatisfactory, the one given in our translation involving a zeugma.

Who a beaker embellished bore with decorum,
40 And gleaming-drink poured. The gleeman sang whilom

Hearty in Heorot ; there was heroes' rejoicing,
A numerous war-band of Weders and Danemen.

IX.

UNFERTII TAUNTS BEOWULF.

Unferth spoke up, Ecglaf his son,
Who sat at the feet of the lord of the Scyldings,
Opened the jousting (the journey[1] of Beowulf,
Sea-farer doughty, gave sorrow to Unferth

5 And greatest chagrin, too, for granted he never
That any man else on earth should attain to,
Gain under heaven, more glory than he) :
" Art thou that Beowulf with Breca did struggle,
On the wide sea-currents at swimming contended,

10 Where to humor your pride the ocean ye tried,
From vainest vaunting adventured your bodies
In care of the waters? And no one was able
Nor lief nor loth one, in the least to dissuade you

Your difficult voyage ; then ye ventured a-swimming,
15 Where your arms outstretching the streams ye did cover,
The mere-ways measured, mixing and stirring them,
Glided the ocean ; angry the waves were,
With the weltering of winter. In the water's possession,
Ye toiled for a seven-night ; he at swimming outdid thee,
20 In strength excelled thee. Then early at morning
On the Heathoremes' shore the holm-currents tossed him,
Sought he thenceward the home of his fathers,
Beloved of his liegemen, the land of the Brondings,
The peace-castle pleasant, where a people he wielded,

---

[1] It has been plausibly suggested that 'sið' (in 501 and in 353) means
'arrival.'   If so, translate the bracket: (*the arrival of Beowulf, the brave
seafarer, was a source of great chagrin to Unferth, etc.*).

25 Had borough and jewels.   The pledge that he made thee

Breca outdid you entirely.

The son of Beanstan hath soothly accomplished.

Then I ween thou wilt find thee less fortunate issue,

Much more will Grendel outdo you, if you vie with him in prowess.

Though ever triumphant in onset of battle,

A grim grappling, if Grendel thou darest

30 For the space of a night near-by to wait for!"

Beowulf retaliates.

Beowulf answered, offspring of Ecgtheow:

" My good friend Unferth, sure freely and wildly,

O friend Unferth, you are fuddled with beer, and cannot talk coherently. 35

Thou fuddled with beer of Breca hast spoken,

Hast told of his journey!   A fact I allege it,

That greater strength in the waters I had then,

Ills in the ocean, than any man else had.

We made agreement as the merest of striplings

Promised each other (both of us then were

We simply kept an engagement made in early life.

Younkers in years) that we yet would adventure

40 Out on the ocean ; it all we accomplished.

While swimming the sea-floods, sword-blade unscabbarded

Boldly we brandished, our bodies expected

To shield from the sharks.   He sure was unable

He could not excel me, and I would not excel him. 45

To swim on the waters further than I could,

More swift on the waves, nor *would* I from him go.

Then we two companions stayed in the ocean

After five days the currents separated us.

Five nights together, till the currents did part us,

The weltering waters, weathers the bleakest,

And nethermost night, and the north-wind whistled

50 Fierce in our faces ; fell were the billows.

The mere fishers' mood was mightily ruffled :

And there against foemen my firm-knotted corslet,

Hand-jointed, hardy, help did afford me ;

My battle-sark braided, brilliantly gilded,

A horrible sea-beast attacked me, but I slew him. 55

Lay on my bosom.   To the bottom then dragged me,

A hateful fiend-scather, seized me and held me,

Grim in his grapple : 'twas granted me, nathless,

To pierce the monster with the point of my weapon,

My obedient blade ; battle offcarried

60 The mighty mere-creature by means of my hand-blow.

X.

BEOWULF SILENCES UNFERTH.—GLEE IS HIGH.

" So ill-meaning enemies often did cause me
Sorrow the sorest, I served them, in quittance,
With my dear-lovèd sword, as in sooth it was fitting;
They missed the pleasure of feasting abundantly,

My dear sword always served me faithfully.

5 Ill-doers evil, of eating my body,
Of surrounding the banquet deep in the ocean;
But wounded with edges early at morning
They were stretched a-high on the strand of the ocean,
Put to sleep with the sword, that sea-going travelers

I put a stop to the outrages of the sea-monsters.

10 No longer thereafter were hindered from sailing
The foam-dashing currents.   Came a light from the east,
God's beautiful beacon; the billows subsided,
That well I could see the nesses projecting,
The blustering crags.   Weird often saveth

Fortune helps the brave earl.

15 The undoomed hero if doughty his valor!
But me did it fortune[1] to fell with my weapon
Nine of the nickers.   Of night-struggle harder
'Neath dome of the heaven heard I but rarely,
Nor of wight more woful in the waves of the ocean;

20 Yet I 'scaped with my life the grip of the monsters,
Weary from travel.   Then the waters bare me
To the land of the Finns, the flood with the current,
The weltering waves.   Not a word hath been told me
Of deeds so daring done by thee, Unferth,

After that escape I drifted to Finland.

I have never heard of your doing any such bold deeds.

25 And of sword-terror none; never hath Breca
At the play of the battle, nor either of you two,
Feat so fearless performèd with weapons
Glinting and gleaming . . . .

---

[1] The repetition of 'hwæðere' (574 and 578) is regarded by some scholars as a defect. B. suggests 'swá þær' for the first: *So there it befell me, etc.* Another suggestion is to change the second 'hwæðere' into 'swá þær': *So there I escaped with my life, etc.*

. . . . I utter no boasting ;

You are a slayer of brothers, and will suffer damnation, wise as you may be.
30 Though with cold-blooded cruelty thou killedst thy brothers,
Thy nearest of kin ; thou needs must in hell get
Direful damnation, though doughty thy wisdom.
I tell thee in earnest, offspring of Ecglaf,
Never had Grendel such numberless horrors,
35 The direful demon, done to thy liegelord,
Harrying in Heorot, if thy heart were as sturdy,

Had your acts been as brave as your words, Grendel had not ravaged your land so long.
Thy mood as ferocious as thou dost describe them.
He hath found out fully that the fierce-burning hatred,
The edge-battle eager, of all of your kindred,
40 Of the Victory-Scyldings, need little dismay him :
Oaths he exacteth, not any he spares

The monster is not afraid of the Danes,
Of the folk of the Danemen, but fighteth with pleasure,
Killeth and feasteth, no contest expecteth

but he will soon learn to dread the Geats.
From Spear-Danish people.   But the prowess and valor
45 Of the earls of the Geatmen early shall venture
To give him a grapple.   He shall go who is able
Bravely to banquet, when the bright-light of morning

On the second day, any warrior may go unmolested to the mead-banquet.
Which the second day bringeth, the sun in its ether-robes,
O'er children of men shines from the southward !"
50 Then the gray-haired, war-famed giver of treasure

Hrothgar's spirits are revived.
Was blithesome and joyous, the Bright-Danish ruler
Expected assistance ; the people's protector

The old king trusts Beowulf. The heroes are joyful.
Heard from Beowulf his bold resolution.
There was laughter of heroes ; loud was the clatter,
55 The words were winsome.   Wealhtheow advanced then,

Queen Wealh- theow plays the hostess.
Consort of Hrothgar, of courtesy mindful,
Gold-decked saluted the men in the building,
And the freeborn woman the beaker presented

She offers the cup to her husband first.
To the lord of the kingdom, first of the East-Danes,
60 Bade him be blithesome when beer was a-flowing,
Lief to his liegemen ; he lustily tasted
Of banquet and beaker, battle-famed ruler.
The Helmingish lady then graciously circled
'Mid all the liegemen lesser and greater :

65 Treasure-cups tendered, till time was afforded
   That the decorous-mooded, diademed folk-queen
   Might bear to Beowulf the bumper o'errunning;
   She greeted the Geat-prince, God she did thank,
   Most wise in her words, that her wish was accomplished,
70 That in any of earlmen she ever should look for
   Solace in sorrow.   He accepted the beaker,
   Battle-bold warrior, at Wealhtheow's giving,
   Then equipped for combat quoth he in measures,
   Beowulf spake, offspring of Ecgtheow:
75 " I purposed in spirit when I mounted the ocean,
   When I boarded my boat with a band of my liegemen,
   I would work to the fullest the will of your people
   Or in foe's-clutches fastened fall in the battle.
   Deeds I shall do of daring and prowess,
80 Or the last of my life-days live in this mead-hall."
   These words to the lady were welcome and pleasing,
   The boast of the Geatman; with gold trappings broidered
   Went the freeborn folk-queen her fond-lord to sit by.
   Then again as of yore was heard in the building
85 Courtly discussion, conquerors' shouting,
   Heroes were happy, till Healfdene's son would
   Go to his slumber to seek for refreshing;
   For the horrid hell-monster in the hall-building knew he
   A fight was determined,[1] since the light of the sun they
90 No longer could see, and lowering darkness
   O'er all had descended, and dark under heaven
   Shadowy shapes came shying around them.
   The liegemen all rose then.   One saluted the other,
   Hrothgar Beowulf, in rhythmical measures,
95 Wishing him well, and, the wassail-hall giving
   To his care and keeping, quoth he departing:

She gives presents to the heroes.

Then she offers the cup to Beowulf, thanking God that aid has come.

Beowulf states to the queen the object of his visit.

I determined to do or die.

Glee is high.

Hrothgar retires, leaving Beowulf in charge of the hall.

---

[1] Kl. suggests a period after 'determined.' This would give the passage
as follows: *Since they no longer could see the light of the sun, and lowering
darkness was down over all, dire under the heavens shadowy beings came going
around them.*

" Not to any one else have I ever entrusted,
But thee and thee only, the hall of the Danemen,
Since high I could heave my hand and my buckler.
100 Take thou in charge now the noblest of houses ;
Be mindful of honor, exhibiting prowess,
Watch 'gainst the foeman !   Thou shalt want no enjoyments,
Survive thou safely adventure so glorious ! "

XI.

ALL SLEEP SAVE ONE.

Hrothgar retires.

Then Hrothgar departed, his earl-throng attending him,
Folk-lord of Scyldings, forth from the building ;
The war-chieftain wished then Wealhtheow to look for,
The queen for a bedmate.   To keep away Grendel

God has provided
a watch for the
hall.

5 The Glory of Kings had given a hall-watch,
As men heard recounted : for the king of the Danemen
He did special service, gave the giant a watcher :
And the prince of the Geatmen implicitly trusted

Beowulf is self-
confident.
He prepares for
rest.

His warlike strength and the Wielder's protection.
10 His armor of iron off him he did then,
His helmet from his head, to his henchman committed
His chased-handled chain-sword, choicest of weapons,
And bade him bide with his battle-equipments.
The good one then uttered words of defiance,

Beowulf boasts of
his ability to cope
with Grendel.

15 Beowulf Geatman, ere his bed he upmounted :
" I hold me no meaner in matters of prowess,
In warlike achievements, than Grendel does himself ;
Hence I seek not with sword-edge to sooth him to slumber.
Of life to bereave him, though well I am able.

We will fight with
nature's weapons
only.

20 No battle-skill[1] has he, that blows he should strike me,
To shatter my shield, though sure he is mighty

---

[1] Gr. understood ' gódra ' as meaning ' advantages in battle.' This rendering H.-So. rejects. The latter takes the passage as meaning that Grendel,
though mighty and formidable, has no skill in the art of war.

In strife and destruction ; but struggling by night we
Shall do without edges, dare he to look for
Weaponless warfare, and wise-mooded Father
25 The glory apportion, God ever-holy,
On which hand soever to him seemeth proper."

God may decide
who shall conquer.

Then the brave-mooded hero bent to his slumber,
The pillow received the cheek of the noble ;
And many a martial mere-thane attending

The Geatish war-
riors lie down.

30 Sank to his slumber.   Seemed it unlikely
That ever thereafter any should hope to
Be happy at home, hero-friends visit
Or the lordly troop-castle where he lived from his childhood ;
They had heard how slaughter had snatched from the wine-hall,

They thought it
very unlikely that
they should ever
see their homes
again.

35 Had recently ravished, of the race of the Scyldings
Too many by far. ' But the Lord to them granted
The weaving of war-speed, to Wederish heroes

But God raised up
a deliverer.

Aid and comfort, that every opponent
By one man's war-might they worsted and vanquished,
40 By the might of himself; the truth is established
That God Almighty hath governed for ages

God rules the
world.

Kindreds and nations.' A night very lurid
The trav'ler-at-twilight came tramping and striding.
The warriors were sleeping who should watch the horned-building,

Grendel comes to
Heorot.

45 One only excepted.   'Mid earthmen 'twas 'stablished,
Th' implacable foeman was powerless to hurl them

Only one warrior
is awake.

To the land of shadows, if the Lord were unwilling ;
But serving as warder, in terror to foemen,
He angrily bided the issue of battle.[1]

---

[1] B. in his masterly articles on Beowulf (P. and B. XII.) rejects the division
usually made at this point. 'þá' (711), usually rendered 'then,' he translates
'when,' and connects its clause with the foregoing sentence. These changes
he makes to reduce the number of 'cóm's' as principal verbs. (Cf. 703, 711,
721.) With all deference to this acute scholar, I must say that it seems to me
that the poet is exhausting his resources to bring out clearly the supreme event
on which the whole subsequent action turns. First, he (Grendel) came *in
the wan night;* second, he came *from the moor ;* third, he came *to the hall.*
Time, place from which, place to which, are all given.

XII.

GRENDEL AND BEOWULF.

Grendel comes
from the fens.

'Neath the cloudy cliffs came from the moor then
Grendel going, God's anger bare he.
The monster intended some one of earthmen
In the hall-building grand to entrap and make way with;

He goes towards
the joyous build-
ing.

5 He went under welkin where well he knew of
The wine-joyous building, brilliant with plating,
Gold-hall of earthmen.   Not the earliest occasion

This was not his
first visit there.

He the home and manor of Hrothgar had sought:
Ne'er found he in life-days later nor earlier
10 Hardier hero, hall-thanes[1] more sturdy!
Then came to the building the warrior marching,

His horrid fingers
tear the door open.

Bereft of his joyance.   The door quickly opened
On fire-hinges fastened, when his fingers had touched it;
The fell one had flung then — his fury so bitter —
15 Open the entrance.   Early thereafter
The foeman trod the shining hall-pavement,

He strides furi-
ously into the hall.

Strode he angrily; from the eyes of him glimmered
A lustre unlovely likest to fire.
He beheld in the hall the heroes in numbers,
20 A circle of kinsmen sleeping together,

He exults over his
supposed prey.

A throng of thanemen: then his thoughts were exultant,
He minded to sunder from each of the thanemen
The life from his body, horrible demon,
Ere morning came, since fate had allowed him

Fate has decreed
that he shall devour
no more heroes.
Beowulf suffers
from suspense.

25 The prospect of plenty.   Providence willed not
To permit him any more of men under heaven
To eat in the night-time.   Higelac's kinsman
Great sorrow endured how the dire-mooded creature

---

[1] B. and t. B. emend so as to make lines 9 and 10 read: *Never in his life,
earlier or later, had he, the hell-thane, found a braver hero.* — They argue
that Beowulf's companions had done nothing to merit such encomiums as the
usual readings allow them.

In unlooked-for assaults were likely to bear him.
30 No thought had the monster of deferring the matter,
But on earliest occasion he quickly laid hold of
A soldier asleep, suddenly tore him,
Bit his bone-prison, the blood drank in currents,
Swallowed in mouthfuls : he soon had the dead man's
35 Feet and hands, too, eaten entirely.
Nearer he strode then, the stout-hearted warrior
Snatched as he slumbered, seizing with hand-grip,
Forward the foeman foined with his hand ;
Caught he quickly the cunning deviser,
40 On his elbow he rested. This early discovered
The master of malice, that in middle-earth's regions,
'Neath the whole of the heavens, no hand-grapple greater
In any man else had he ever encountered :
Fearful in spirit, faint-mooded waxed he,
45 Not off could betake him; death he was pondering,
Would fly to his covert, seek the devils' assembly :
His calling no more was the same he had followed
Long in his lifetime. The liege-kinsman worthy
Of Higelac minded his speech of the evening,
50 Stood he up straight and stoutly did seize him.
His fingers crackled ; the giant was outward,
The earl stepped farther. The famous one minded
To flee away farther, if he found an occasion,
And off and away, avoiding delay,
55 To fly to the fen-moors ; he fully was ware of
The strength of his grapple in the grip of the foeman.
'Twas an ill-taken journey that the injury-bringing,
Harrying harmer to Heorot wandered :
The palace re-echoed ; to all of the Danemen,
60 Dwellers in castles, to each of the bold ones,
Earlmen, was terror. Angry they both were,
Archwarders raging.[1] Rattled the building ;

Grendel immediately seizes a sleeping warrior, and devours him.

Beowulf and Grendel grapple.

The monster is amazed at Beowulf's strength.

He is anxious to flee.

Beowulf recalls his boast of the evening, and determines to fulfil it.

'Twas a luckless day for Grendel.

The hall groans.

[1] For 'réðe rén-weardas' (771), t. B. suggests 'réðc, rénhearde.' Translate: *They were both angry, raging and mighty.*

'Twas a marvellous wonder that the wine-hall withstood then
The bold-in-battle, bent not to earthward,
65 Excellent earth-hall; but within and without it
Was fastened so firmly in fetters of iron,
By the art of the armorer. Off from the sill there
Bent mead-benches many, as men have informed me,
Adorned with gold-work, where the grim ones did struggle.
70 The Scylding wise men weened ne'er before
That by might and main-strength a man under heaven
Might break it in pieces, bone-decked, resplendent,
Crush it by cunning, unless clutch of the fire
In smoke should consume it. The sound mounted upward

Grendel's cries ter-
rify the Danes.
75 Novel enough; on the North Danes fastened
A terror of anguish, on all of the men there
Who heard from the wall the weeping and plaining,
The song of defeat from the foeman of heaven,
Heard him hymns of horror howl, and his sorrow
80 Hell-bound bewailing. He held him too firmly
Who was strongest of main-strength of men of that era.

XIII.

GRENDEL IS VANQUISHED.

Beowulf has no
idea of letting
Grendel live.
For no cause whatever would the earlmen's defender
Leave in life-joys the loathsome newcomer,
He deemed his existence utterly useless
To men under heaven. Many a noble
5 Of Beowulf brandished his battle-sword old,
Would guard the life of his lord and protector,
The far-famous chieftain, if able to do so;
While waging the warfare, this wist they but little,
Brave battle-thanes, while his body intending

No weapon would
harm Grendel; he
bore a charmed
life.
10 To slit into slivers, and seeking his spirit:
That the relentless foeman nor finest of weapons
Of all on the earth, nor any of war-bills

Was willing to injure ; but weapons of victory
Swords and suchlike he had sworn to dispense with.
15 His death at that time must prove to be wretched,
And the far-away spirit widely should journey
Into enemies' power. This plainly he saw then
Who with mirth [1] of mood malice no little
Had wrought in the past on the race of the earthmen
20 (To God he was hostile), that his body would fail him,
But Higelac's hardy henchman and kinsman
Held him by the hand ; hateful to other
Was each one if living. A body-wound suffered
The direful demon, damage incurable

Grendel is sorely wounded.

25 Was seen on his shoulder, his sinews were shivered,

His body bursts.

His body did burst. To Beowulf was given
Glory in battle ; Grendel from thenceward
Must flee and hide him in the fen-cliffs and marshes,
Sick unto death, his dwelling must look for
30 Unwinsome and woful ; he wist the more fully
The end of his earthly existence was nearing,

The monster flees away to hide in the moors.

His life-days' limits. At last for the Danemen,
When the slaughter was over, their wish was accomplished.
The comer-from-far-land had cleansed then of evil,
35 Wise and valiant, the war-hall of Hrothgar,
Saved it from violence. He joyed in the night-work,
In repute for prowess ; the prince of the Geatmen
For the East-Danish people his boast had accomplished,
Bettered their burdensome bale-sorrows fully,
40 The craft-begot evil they erstwhile had suffered
And were forced to endure from crushing oppression,
Their manifold misery. 'Twas a manifest token,
When the hero-in-battle the hand suspended,

Beowulf suspends Grendel's hand and arm in Heorot.

The arm and the shoulder (there was all of the claw
45 Of Grendel together) 'neath great-stretching hall-roof.

---

[1] It has been proposed to translate 'myrðe' by *with sorrow ;* but there seems no authority for such a rendering. To the present translator, the phrase 'módes myrðe' seems a mere padding for *gladly ;* i.e., *he who gladly harassed mankind.*

XIV.

REJOICING OF THE DANES.

At early dawn,
warriors from far
and near come to-
gether to hear of
the night's adven-
tures.

Few warriors la-
mented Grendel's
destruction.

Grendel's blood
dyes the waters.

Beowulf is the hero
of the hour.

He is regarded as a
probable successor
to Hrothgar.

But no word is
uttered to derogate
from the old king.

In the mist of the morning many a warrior
Stood round the gift-hall, as the story is told me :
Folk-princes fared then from far and from near
Through long-stretching journeys to look at the wonder,
5   The footprints of the foeman.   Few of the warriors
Who gazed on the foot-tracks of the inglorious creature
His parting from life pained very deeply,
How, weary in spirit, off from those regions
In combats conquered he carried his traces,
10 Fated and flying, to the flood of the nickers.
There in bloody billows bubbled the currents,
The angry eddy was everywhere mingled
And seething with gore, welling with sword-blood ;[1]
He death-doomed had hid him, when reaved of his joyance
15 He laid down his life in the lair he had fled to,
His heathenish spirit, where hell did receive him.
Thence the friends from of old backward turned them,
And many a younker from merry adventure,
Striding their stallions, stout from the seaward,
20 Heroes on horses.   There were heard very often
Beowulf's praises ; many often asserted
That neither south nor north, in the circuit of waters,
O'er outstretching earth-plain, none other was better
'Mid bearers of war-shields, more worthy to govern,
25 'Neath the arch of the ether.   Not any, however,
'Gainst the friend-lord muttered, mocking-words uttered
Of Hrothgar the gracious (a good king he).
Oft the famed ones permitted their fallow-skinned horses

---

[1] S. emends, suggesting 'déop' for 'déog,' and removing semicolon after
'wéol.' The two half-lines 'welling . . . hid him' would then read: *The
bloody deep welled with sword-gore.* B. accepts 'déop' for 'déog,' but reads
'déað-fæges': *The deep boiled with the sword-gore of the death-doomed one.*

To run in rivalry, racing and chasing,
30 Where the fieldways appeared to them fair and inviting,
Known for their excellence ; oft a thane of the folk-lord,[1]
[2] A man of celebrity, mindful of rhythms,
Who ancient traditions treasured in memory,
New word-groups found properly bound :
35 The bard after 'gan then Beowulf's venture
Wisely to tell of, and words that were clever
To utter skilfully, earnestly speaking,
Everything told he that he heard as to Sigmund's
Mighty achievements, many things hidden,
40 The strife of the Wælsing, the wide-going ventures
The children of men knew of but little,
The feud and the fury, but Fitela with him,
When suchlike matters he minded to speak of,
Uncle to nephew, as in every contention
45 Each to other was ever devoted :
A numerous host of the race of the scathers
They had slain with the sword-edge. To Sigmund accrued then
No little of glory, when his life-days were over,
Since he sturdy in struggle had destroyed the great dragon,
50 The hoard-treasure's keeper ; 'neath the hoar-grayish stone he,
The son of the atheling, unaided adventured
The perilous project ; not present was Fitela,
Yet the fortune befell him of forcing his weapon
Through the marvellous dragon, that it stood in the wall,
55 Well-honored weapon ; the worm was yslaughtered.
The great one had gained then by his glorious achievement
To reap from the ring-hoard richest enjoyment,

The gleeman sings the deeds of heroes.

He sings in alliterative measures of Beowulf's prowess.

Also of Sigemund, who had slain a great fire-drake.

---

[1] Another and quite different rendering of this passage is as follows: *Oft a liegeman of the king, a fame-covered man mindful of songs, who very many ancient traditions remembered (he found other word-groups accurately bound together) began afterward to tell of Beowulf's adventure, skilfully to narrate it, etc.*

[2] Might ' guma gilp-hladen ' mean ' a man laden with boasts of the deeds of others'?

As best it did please him : his vessel he loaded,
Shining ornaments on the ship's bosom carried,
60 Kinsman of Wæls : the drake in heat melted.

Sigemund was
widely famed.

He was farthest famed of fugitive pilgrims,
Mid wide-scattered world-folk, for works of great prowess,
War-troopers' shelter : hence waxed he in honor.[1]

Heremod, an un-
fortunate Danish
king, is introduced
by way of contrast.

Afterward Heremod's hero-strength failed him,
65 His vigor and valor. 'Mid venomous haters
To the hands of foemen he was foully delivered,
Offdriven early. Agony-billows

Unlike Sigemund
and Beowulf, Here-
mod was a burden
to his people.

Oppressed him too long, to his people he became then,
To all the athelings, an ever-great burden ;
70 And the daring one's journey in days of yore
Many wise men were wont to deplore,
Such as hoped he would bring them help in their sorrow,
That the son of their ruler should rise into power,
Holding the headship held by his fathers,
75 Should govern the people, the gold-hoard and borough,
The kingdom of heroes, the realm of the Scyldings.

Beowulf is an
honor to his race.

He to all men became then far more beloved,
Higelac's kinsman, to kindreds and races,
To his friends much dearer ; him malice assaulted. —

The story is re-
sumed.

80 Oft running and racing on roadsters they measured
The dun-colored highways. Then the light of the morning
Was hurried and hastened. Went henchmen in numbers
To the beautiful building, bold ones in spirit,
To look at the wonder ; the liegelord himself then
85 From his wife-bower wending, warden of treasures,
Glorious trod with troopers unnumbered,
Famed for his virtues, and with him the queen-wife
Measured the mead-ways, with maidens attending.

[1] t. B. accepts B.'s ' hé þæs áron þáh ' as given by H.-So., but puts a comma
after ' þáh,' and takes 'siððan ' as introducing a dependent clause : *He throve
in honor since Heremod's strength . . . had decreased.*

XV.

HROTHGAR'S GRATITUDE.

Hrothgar discoursed (to the hall-building went he,
He stood by the pillar,[1] saw the steep-rising hall-roof
Gleaming with gold-gems, and Grendel his hand there) :
" For the sight we behold now, thanks to the Wielder
5 Early be offered !   Much evil I bided,
Snaring from Grendel :[2] God can e'er 'complish
Wonder on wonder, Wielder of Glory !
But lately I reckoned ne'er under heaven
Comfort to gain me for any of sorrows,
10 While the handsomest of houses horrid with bloodstain
Gory uptowered ; grief had offfrightened[3]
Each of the wise ones who weened not that ever
The folk-troop's defences 'gainst foes they should strengthen,
'Gainst sprites and monsters. Through the might of the Wielder
15 A doughty retainer hath a deed now accomplished
Which erstwhile we all with our excellent wisdom
Failed to perform.   May affirm very truly
What woman soever in all of the nations
Gave birth to the child, if yet she surviveth,
20 That the long-ruling Lord was lavish to herward
In the birth of the bairn.   Now, Beowulf dear,
Most excellent hero, I'll love thee in spirit
As bairn of my body ; bear well henceforward
The relationship new.   No lack shall befall thee
25 Of earth-joys any I ever can give thee.
Full often for lesser service I've given

Hrothgar gives thanks for the overthrow of the monster.

I had given up all hope, when this brave liegeman came to our aid.

If his mother yet liveth, well may she thank God for this son.

Hereafter, Beowulf, thou shalt be my son.

---

[1] B. and t. B. read 'staþole,' and translate *stood on the floor.*

[2] For 'snaring from Grendel,' 'sorrows at Grendel's hands' has been suggested. This gives a parallel to 'láðes.' 'Grynna' may well be gen. pl. of 'gyrn,' by a scribal slip.

[3] The H.-So. punctuation has been followed; but B. has been followed in understanding 'gehwylcne' as object of 'wid-scofen (hæfde).' Gr. construes 'wéa' as nom. abs.

Hero less hardy hoard-treasure precious,

To a weaker in war-strife.   By works of distinction
Thou hast gained for thyself now that thy glory shall flourish
30 Forever and ever.   The All-Ruler quite thee
With good from His hand as He hitherto did thee ! "

Beowulf answered, Ecgtheow's offspring :
" That labor of glory most gladly achieved we,
The combat accomplished, unquailing we ventured
35 The enemy's grapple ; I would grant it much rather
Thou wert able to look at the creature in person,
Faint unto falling, the foe in his trappings !
On murder-bed quickly I minded to bind him,
With firm-holding fetters, that forced by my grapple
40 Low he should lie in life-and-death struggle
'Less his body escape ; I was wholly unable,

Since God did not will it, to keep him from going,
Not held him that firmly, hated opposer ;
Too swift was the foeman.   Yet safety regarding
45 He suffered his hand behind him to linger,
His arm and shoulder, to act as watcher ;

No shadow of solace the woe-begone creature
Found him there nathless : the hated destroyer
Liveth no longer, lashed for his evils,
50 But sorrow hath seized him, in snare-meshes hath him
Close in its clutches, keepeth him writhing
In baleful bonds : there banished for evil
The man shall wait for the mighty tribunal,

How the God of glory shall give him his earnings."
55 Then the soldier kept silent, son of old Ecglaf,

From boasting and bragging of battle-achievements,
Since the princes beheld there the hand that depended
'Neath the lofty hall-timbers by the might of the nobleman,
Each one before him, the enemy's fingers ;
60 Each finger-nail strong steel most resembled,
The heathen one's hand-spur, the hero-in-battle's
Claw most uncanny ; quoth they agreeing,

That not any excellent edges of brave ones   No sword will
                                                              harm the monster.
     Was willing to touch him, the terrible creature's
65   Battle-hand bloody to bear away from him.

XVI.

HROTHGAR LAVISHES GIFTS UPON HIS DELIVERER.

Then straight was ordered that Heorot inside [1]   Heorot is adorned
                                                             with hands.
With hands be embellished : a host of them gathered,
Of men and women, who the wassailing-building
The guest-hall begeared.   Gold-flashing sparkled
5   Webs on the walls then, of wonders a many
To each of the heroes that look on such objects.
The beautiful building was broken to pieces   The hall is defaced,
                                                             however.
Which all within with irons was fastened,
Its hinges torn off : only the roof was
10   Whole and uninjured when the horrible creature
Outlawed for evil off had betaken him,
Hopeless of living.   'Tis hard to avoid it
(Whoever will do it !) ; but he doubtless must come to [2]   [A vague passage
                                                             of five verses.]
The place awaiting, as Wyrd hath appointed,
15   Soul-bearers, earth-dwellers, earls under heaven,
Where bound on its bed his body shall slumber
When feasting is finished.   Full was the time then   Hrothgar goes to
                                                             the banquet.
That the son of Healfdene went to the building ;

[1] Kl. suggests 'hroden' for 'háten,' and renders: *Then quickly was
Heorot adorned within, with hands bedecked.* — B. suggests 'gefrætwon' instead of 'gefrætwod,' and renders : *Then was it commanded to adorn Heorot
within quickly with hands.* — The former has the advantage of affording a
parallel to 'gefrætwod': both have the disadvantage of altering the text.

[2] The passage 1005–1009 seems to be hopeless.   One difficult point is to
find a subject for 'gesacan.'   Some say 'he'; others supply 'each,' *i.e., every
soul-bearer . . . must gain the inevitable place.*   The genitives in this case are
partitive. — If 'he' be subj., the genitives are dependent on 'gearwe' (= prepared). — The 'he' itself is disputed, some referring it to Grendel; but B.
takes it as involved in the parenthesis.

The excellent atheling would eat of the banquet.
20 Ne'er heard I that people with hero-band larger
Bare them better tow'rds their bracelet-bestower.
The laden-with-glory stooped to the bench then
(Their kinsmen-companions in plenty were joyful,
Many a cupful quaffing complaisantly),
25 Doughty of spirit in the high-tow'ring palace,

Hrothgar's nephew, Hrothulf, is present.

Hrothgar and Hrothulf.   Heorot then inside
Was filled with friendly ones; falsehood and treachery
The Folk-Scyldings now nowise did practise.

Hrothgar lavishes gifts upon Beowulf.

Then the offspring of Healfdene offered to Beowulf
30 A golden standard, as reward for the victory,
A banner embossed, burnie and helmet;
Many men saw then a song-famous weapon
Borne 'fore the hero.   Beowulf drank of
The cup in the building; that treasure-bestowing
35 He needed not blush for in battle-men's presence.

Four handsomer gifts were never presented.

Ne'er heard I that many men on the ale-bench
In friendlier fashion to their fellows presented
Four bright jewels with gold-work embellished.
'Round the roof of the helmet a head-guarder outside
40 Braided with wires, with bosses was furnished,
That swords-for-the-battle fight-hardened might fail
Boldly to harm him, when the hero proceeded

Hrothgar commands that eight finely caparisoned steeds be brought to Beowulf.

Forth against foemen.   The defender of earls then
Commanded that eight steeds with bridles
45 Gold-plated, gleaming, be guided to hallward,
Inside the building; on one of them stood then
An art-broidered saddle embellished with jewels;
'Twas the sovereign's seat, when the son of King Healfdene
Was pleased to take part in the play of the edges;
50 The famous one's valor ne'er failed at the front when
Slain ones were bowing.   And to Beowulf granted
The prince of the Ingwins, power over both,
O'er war-steeds and weapons; bade him well to enjoy them.
In so manly a manner the mighty-famed chieftain,

55 Hoard-ward of heroes, with horses and jewels
War-storms requited, that none e'er condemneth
Who willeth to tell truth with full justice.

XVII.

BANQUET (*continued*).—THE SCOP'S SONG OF FINN AND HNÆF.

And the atheling of earlmen to each of the heroes
Who the ways of the waters went with Beowulf,
A costly gift-token gave on the mead-bench,
Offered an heirloom, and ordered that that man
5 With gold should be paid for, whom Grendel had erstwhile
Wickedly slaughtered, as he more of them had done
Had far-seeing God and the mood of the hero
The fate not averted : the Father then governed
All of the earth-dwellers, as He ever is doing ;
10 Hence insight for all men is everywhere fittest,
Forethought of spirit ! much he shall suffer
Of lief and of loathsome who long in this present
Useth the world in this woful existence.
There was music and merriment mingling together
15 Touching Healfdene's leader ; the joy-wood was fingered,
Measures recited, when the singer of Hrothgar
On mead-bench should mention the merry hall-joyance
Of the kinsmen of Finn, when onset surprised them :
"The Half-Danish hero, Hnæf of the Scyldings,
20 On the field of the Frisians was fated to perish,
Sure Hildeburg needed not mention approving
The faith of the Jutemen : though blameless entirely,
When shields were shivered she was shorn of her darlings,
Of bairns and brothers : they bent to their fate
25 With war-spear wounded ; woe was that woman.
Not causeless lamented the daughter of Hoce
The decree of the Wielder when morning-light came and
She was able 'neath heaven to behold the destruction

Each of Beowulf's companions receives a costly gift.

The warrior killed by Grendel is to be paid for in gold.

Hrothgar's scop recalls events in the reign of his lord's father.

Hnæf, the Danish general, is treacherously attacked while staying at Finn's castle.

Queen Hildeburg is not only wife of Finn, but a kinswoman of the murdered Hnæf.

Of brothers and bairns, where the brightest of earth-joys

Finn's force is al- 30
most exterminated.
She had hitherto had : all the henchmen of Finn
War had offtaken, save a handful remaining,
That he nowise was able to offer resistance [1]

Hengest succeeds
Hnæf as Danish
general.
To the onset of Hengest in the parley of battle,
Nor the wretched remnant to rescue in war from

35 The earl of the atheling ; but they offered conditions,

Compact between
the Frisians and the
Danes.
Another great building to fully make ready,
A hall and a high-seat, that half they might rule with
The sons of the Jutemen, and that Folcwalda's son would
Day after day the Danemen honor

40 When gifts were giving, and grant of his ring-store
To Hengest's earl-troop ever so freely,
Of his gold-plated jewels, as he encouraged the Frisians

Equality of gifts
agreed on.
On the bench of the beer-hall. On both sides they swore then
A fast-binding compact ; Finn unto Hengest

45 With no thought of revoking vowed then most solemnly
The woe-begone remnant well to take charge of,
His Witan advising ; the agreement should no one
By words or works weaken and shatter,
By artifice ever injure its value,

50 Though reaved of their ruler their ring-giver's slayer
They followed as vassals, Fate so requiring :

No one shall refer
to old grudges.
Then if one of the Frisians the quarrel should speak of
In tones that were taunting, terrible edges
Should cut in requital. Accomplished the oath was,

55 And treasure of gold from the hoard was unlifted.

Danish warriors
are burned on a
funeral-pyre.
The best of the Scylding braves was then fully
Prepared for the pile ; at the pyre was seen clearly
The blood-gory burnie, the boar with his gilding,
The iron-hard swine, athelings many

60 Fatally wounded ; no few had been slaughtered.
Hildeburg bade then, at the burning of Hnæf,

---

[1] For 1084, R. suggests ' wiht Hengeste wið gefeohtan.' — K. suggests ' wið
Hengeste wiht gefeohtan.' Neither emendation would make any essential
change in the translation.

The bairn of her bosom to bear to the fire,
That his body be burned and borne to the pyre.
The woe-stricken woman wept on his shoulder,[1]
65 In measures lamented ; upmounted the hero.[2]
The greatest of dead-fires curled to the welkin,
On the hill's-front crackled ; heads were a-melting,
Wound-doors bursting, while the blood was a-coursing
From body-bite fierce. The fire devoured them,
70 Greediest of spirits, whom war had offcarried
From both of the peoples ; their bravest were fallen.

Queen Hildeburg has her son burnt along with Hnæf.

XVIII.

THE FINN EPISODE (*continued*).— THE BANQUET CONTINUES.

" Then the warriors departed to go to their dwellings,
Reaved of their friends, Friesland to visit,
Their homes and high-city. Hengest continued
Biding with Finn the blood-tainted winter,
5 Wholly unsundered ;[3] of fatherland thought he
Though unable to drive the ring-stemmèd vessel

The survivors go to Friesland, the home of Finn.

Hengest remains there all winter, unable to get away.

---

[1] The separation of adjective and noun by a phrase (cf. v. 1118) being very unusual, some scholars have put 'earme on eaxle' with the foregoing lines, inserting a semicolon after 'eaxle.' In this case 'on eaxe' (*i.e.*, on the ashes, cinders) is sometimes read, and this affords a parallel to 'on bæl.' Let us hope that a satisfactory rendering will yet be reached without resorting to any tampering with the text, such as Lichtenheld proposed : 'earme ides on eaxle gnornode.'

[2] For 'gáð-rinc,' 'gáð-réc,' *battle-smoke*, has been suggested.

[3] For 1130 (1) R. and Gr. suggest 'elne unflitme' as 1098 (1) reads. The latter verse is undisputed ; and, for the former, 'elne' would be as possible as 'ealles,' and 'unflitme' is well supported. Accepting 'elne unflitme' for both, I would suggest '*very peaceably*' for both places : (1) *Finn to Hengest very peaceably vowed with oaths, etc.* (2) *Hengest then still the slaughter-stained winter remained there with Finn very peaceably.* The two passages become thus correlatives, the second a sequel of the first. 'Elne,' in the sense of very (swíðe), needs no argument ; and 'unflitme' (from 'flítan') can, it seems to me, be more plausibly rendered 'peaceful,' 'peaceable,' than 'contestable,' or 'conquerable.'

O'er the ways of the waters; the wave-deeps were tossing,
Fought with the wind; winter in ice-bonds
Closed up the currents, till there came to the dwelling
10 A year in its course, as yet it revolveth,
If season propitious one alway regardeth,
World-cheering weathers. Then winter was gone,
Earth's bosom was lovely; the exile would get him,

He devises
schemes of ven-
geance.
The guest from the palace; on grewsomest vengeance
15 He brooded more eager than on oversea journeys,
Whe'r onset-of-anger he were able to 'complish,
The bairns of the Jutemen therein to remember.
Nowise refused he the duties of liegeman
When Hun of the Frisians the battle-sword Láfing,
20 Fairest of falchions, friendly did give him:
Its edges were famous in folk-talk of Jutland.
And savage sword-fury seized in its clutches
Bold-mooded Finn where he bode in his palace,

Guthlaf and Oslaf
revenge Hnæf's
slaughter.
When the grewsome grapple Guthlaf and Oslaf
25 Had mournfully mentioned, the mere-journey over,
For sorrows half-blamed him; the flickering spirit
Could not bide in his bosom. Then the building was covered [1]

Finn is slain.
With corpses of foemen, and Finn too was slaughtered,
The king with his comrades, and the queen made a prisoner.

The jewels of Finn,
and his queen are
carried away by
the Danes.
30 The troops of the Scyldings bore to their vessels
All that the land-king had in his palace,
Such trinkets and treasures they took as, on searching,
At Finn's they could find. They ferried to Daneland
The excellent woman on oversea journey,

The lay is con-
cluded, and the
main story is re-
sumed.
35 Led her to their land-folk." The lay was concluded,
The gleeman's recital. Shouts again rose then,
Bench-glee resounded, bearers then offered

Skinkers carry
round the beaker.
Wine from wonder-vats. Wealhtheo advanced then
Going 'neath gold-crown, where the good ones were seated

---

[1] Some scholars have proposed 'roden'; the line would then read: *Then the building was reddened, etc.*, instead of 'covered.' The 'h' may have been carried over from the three alliterating 'h's.'

40 Uncle and nephew; their peace was yet mutual,
True each to the other.   And Unferth the spokesman
Sat at the feet of the lord of the Scyldings:
Each trusted his spirit that his mood was courageous,
Though at fight he had failed in faith to his kinsmen.

45 Said the queen of the Scyldings : " My lord and protector,
Treasure-bestower, take thou this beaker ;
Joyance attend thee, gold-friend of heroes,
And greet thou the Geatmen with gracious responses !
So ought one to do.   Be kind to the Geatmen,

50 In gifts not niggardly ; anear and afar now
Peace thou enjoyest.   Report hath informed me
Thou'lt have for a bairn the battle-brave hero.
Now is Heorot cleansèd, ring-palace gleaming ;
Give while thou mayest many rewards,

55 And bequeath to thy kinsmen kingdom and people,
On wending thy way to the Wielder's splendor.
I know good Hrothulf, that the noble young troopers
He'll care for and honor, lord of the Scyldings,
If earth-joys thou endest earlier than he doth ;

60 I reckon that recompense he'll render with kindness
Our offspring and issue, if that all he remember,
What favors of yore, when he yet was an infant,
We awarded to him for his worship and pleasure."
Then she turned by the bench where her sons were carousing,

65 Hrethric and Hrothmund, and the heroes' offspring,
The war-youth together ; there the good one was sitting
'Twixt the brothers twain, Beowulf Geatman.

Queen Wealh-
theow greets
Hrothgar, as he
sits beside Hroth-
ulf, his nephew.

Be generous to
the Geats.

Have as much joy
as possible in thy
hall, once more
purified.

I know that Hroth-
ulf will prove faith-
ful if he survive
thee.

Beowulf is sitting
by the two royal
sons.

XIX.

BEOWULF RECEIVES FURTHER HONOR.

A beaker was borne him, and bidding to quaff it
Graciously given, and gold that was twisted
Pleasantly proffered, a pair of arm-jewels,

More gifts are of-
fered Beowulf.

Rings and corslet, of collars the greatest
5 I've heard of 'neath heaven.   Of heroes not any
More splendid from jewels have I heard 'neath the welkin,

A famous necklace
is referred to, in
comparison with
the gems presented
to Beowulf.

Since Hama offbore the Brosingmen's necklace,
The bracteates and jewels, from the bright-shining city,[1]
Eormenric's cunning craftiness fled from,
10 Chose gain everlasting.   Geatish Higelac,
Grandson of Swerting, last had this jewel
When tramping 'neath banner the treasure he guarded,
The field-spoil defended ; Fate offcarried him
When for deeds of daring he endured tribulation,
15 Hate from the Frisians ; the ornaments bare he
O'er the cup of the currents, costly gem-treasures,
Mighty folk-leader, he fell 'neath his target ;
The [2] corpse of the king then came into charge of
The race of the Frankmen, the mail-shirt and collar :
20 Warmen less noble plundered the fallen,
When the fight was finished ; the folk of the Geatmen
The field of the dead held in possession.
The choicest of mead-halls with cheering resounded.
Wealhtheo discoursed, the war-troop addressed she :

Queen Wealh-
theow magnifies
Beowulf's achieve-
ments.

25 "This collar enjoy thou, Beowulf worthy,
Young man, in safety, and use thou this armor,
Gems of the people, and prosper thou fully,
Show thyself sturdy and be to these liegemen
Mild with instruction ! I'll mind thy requital.
30 Thou hast brought it to pass that far and near
Forever and ever earthmen shall honor thee,
Even so widely as ocean surroundeth
The blustering bluffs. Be, while thou livest,

---

[1] C. suggests a semicolon after 'city,' with 'he' as supplied subject of
'fled' and 'chose.'

[2] For 'feorh' S. suggests 'feoh': 'corpse' in the translation would then
be changed to '*possessions*,' '*belongings*.' This is a better reading than one
joining, in such intimate syntactical relations, things so unlike as 'corpse' and
'jewels.'

A wealth-blessèd atheling. I wish thee most truly
35 Jewels and treasure. Be kind to my son, thou
   Living in joyance ! Here each of the nobles
   Is true unto other, gentle in spirit,
   Loyal to leader. The liegemen are peaceful,
   The war-troops ready : well-drunken heroes,[1]
40 Do as I bid ye." Then she went to the settle.
   There was choicest of banquets, wine drank the heroes :
   Weird they knew not, destiny cruel,
   As to many an earlman early it happened,
   When evening had come and Hrothgar had parted
45 Off to his manor, the mighty to slumber.
   Warriors unnumbered warded the building
   As erst they did often : the ale-settle bared they,
   'Twas covered all over with beds and pillows.
   Doomed unto death, down to his slumber
50 Bowed then a beer-thane. Their battle-shields placed they,
   Bright-shining targets, up by their heads then ;
   O'er the atheling on ale-bench 'twas easy to see there
   Battle-high helmet, burnie of ring-mail,
   And mighty war-spear. 'Twas the wont of that people
55 To constantly keep them equipped for the battle,[2]
   At home or marching — in either condition —
   At seasons just such as necessity ordered
   As best for their ruler ; that people was worthy.

May gifts never fail thee.

They little know of the sorrow in store for them.

A doomed thane is there with them.

They were always ready for battle.

---

[1] S. suggests '*wine-joyous heroes,*' '*warriors elated with wine.*'

[2] I believe this translation brings out the meaning of the poet, without departing seriously from the H.-So. text. 'Oft' frequently means 'constantly,' 'continually,' not always 'often.' — Why 'an (on) wig gearwe' should be written 'ánwig-gearwe' (= ready for single combat), I cannot see. 'Gearwe' occurs quite frequently with 'on'; cf. B. 1110 (*ready for the pyre*), El. 222 (*ready for the glad journey*). Moreover, what has the idea of single combat to do with B. 1247 ff.? The poet is giving an inventory of the arms and armor which they lay aside on retiring, and he closes his narration by saying that they were *always prepared for battle both at home and on the march.*

XX.

THE MOTHER OF GRENDEL.

They sank then to slumber.   With sorrow one paid for
His evening repose, as often betid them
While Grendel was holding [1] the gold-bedecked palace,
Ill-deeds performing, till his end overtook him,

Grendel's mother is known to be thirsting for revenge.

5   Death for his sins.   'Twas seen very clearly,
Known unto earth-folk, that still an avenger
Outlived the loathed one, long since the sorrow
Caused by the struggle ; the mother of Grendel,
Devil-shaped woman, her woe ever minded,

[Grendel's progenitor, Cain, is again referred to.]

10 Who was held to inhabit the horrible waters,
The cold-flowing currents, after Cain had become a
Slayer-with-edges to his one only brother,
The son of his sire ; he set out then banished,
Marked as a murderer, man-joys avoiding,

The poet again magnifies Beowulf's valor.

15 Lived in the desert.   Thence demons unnumbered
Fate-sent awoke ; one of them Grendel,
Sword-cursèd, hateful, who at Heorot met with
A man that was watching, waiting the struggle,
Where a horrid one held him with hand-grapple sturdy ;
20 Nathless he minded the might of his body,
The glorious gift God had allowed him,
And folk-ruling Father's favor relied on,
His help and His comfort : so he conquered the foeman,
The hell-spirit humbled : he unhappy departed then,
25 Reaved of his joyance, journeying to death-haunts,
Foeman of man.   His mother moreover

Grendel's mother comes to avenge her son.

Eager and gloomy was anxious to go on
Her mournful mission, mindful of vengeance
For the death of her son.   She came then to Heorot

---

[1] Several eminent authorities either read or emend the MS. so as to make
this verse read, *While Grendel was wasting the gold-bedecked palace.* So 20,15
below : *ravaged the desert.*

30 Where the Armor-Dane earlmen all through the building
Were lying in slumber. Soon there became then
Return[1] to the nobles, when the mother of Grendel
Entered the folk-hall; the fear was less grievous
By even so much as the vigor of maidens,
35 War-strength of women, by warrior is reckoned,
When well-carved weapon, worked with the hammer,
Blade very bloody, brave with its edges,
Strikes down the boar-sign that stands on the helmet.
Then the hard-edgèd weapon was heard in the building,[2]
40 The brand o'er the benches, broad-lindens many
Hand-fast were lifted; for helmet he recked not,
For armor-net broad, whom terror laid hold of.
She went then hastily, outward would get her
Her life for to save, when some one did spy her;
45 Soon she had grappled one of the athelings

She seizes a favorite liegemen of Hrothgar's.

Fast and firmly, when fenward she hied her;
That one to Hrothgar was liefest of heroes
In rank of retainer where waters encircle,
A mighty shield-warrior, whom she murdered at slumber,
50 A broadly-famed battle-knight. Beowulf was absent,
But another apartment was erstwhile devoted

Beowulf was asleep in another part of the palace.

To the glory-decked Geatman when gold was distributed.
There was hubbub in Heorot. The hand that was famous
She grasped in its gore;[3] grief was renewed then

---

[1] For 'sóna' (1281), t. B. suggests 'sára,' limiting 'edhwyrft.' Read then: *Return of sorrows to the nobles, etc.* This emendation supplies the syntactical gap after 'edhwyrft.'

[2] Some authorities follow Grein's lexicon in treating 'heard-ecg' as an adj. limiting 'sweord': II.-So. renders it as a subst. (So v. 1491.) The sense of the translation would be the same.

[3] B. suggests 'under hróf genam' (v. 1303). This emendation, as well as an emendation with (?) to v. 739, he offers, because 'under' baffles him in both passages. All we need is to take 'under' in its secondary meaning of 'in,' which, though not given by Grein, occurs in the literature. Cf. Chron. 876 (March's A.-S. Gram. § 355) and Oro. Amaz. I. 10, where 'under'= *in the midst of.* Cf. modern Eng. 'in such circumstances,' which interchanges in good usage with 'under such circumstances.'

55 In homes and houses : 'twas no happy arrangement
In both of the quarters to barter and purchase
With lives of their friends.   Then the well-agèd ruler,
The gray-headed war-thane, was woful in spirit,
When his long-trusted liegeman lifeless he knew of,

Beowulf is sent for.

60 His dearest one gone.   Quick from a room was
Beowulf brought, brave and triumphant.
As day was dawning in the dusk of the morning,

He comes at Hrothgar's summons.

Went then that earlman, champion noble,
Came with comrades, where the clever one bided
65 Whether God all gracious would grant him a respite
After the woe he had suffered.   The war-worthy hero
With a troop of retainers trod then the pavement
(The hall-building groaned), till he greeted the wise one,

Beowulf inquires how Hrothgar had enjoyed his night's rest.

The earl of the Ingwins;[1] asked if the night had
70 Fully refreshed him, as fain he would have it.

XXI.

HROTHGAR'S ACCOUNT OF THE MONSTERS.

Hrothgar laments the death of Æschere, his shoulder-companion.

Hrothgar rejoined, helm of the Scyldings :
" Ask not of joyance !   Grief is renewed to
The folk of the Danemen.   Dead is Æschere,
Yrmenlaf's brother, older than he,
5 My true-hearted counsellor, trusty adviser,
Shoulder-companion, when fighting in battle
Our heads we protected, when troopers were clashing,

He was my ideal hero.

And heroes were dashing ; such an earl should be ever,
An erst-worthy atheling, as Æschere proved him.
10 The flickering death-spirit became in Heorot
His hand-to-hand murderer ; I can not tell whither
The cruel one turned in the carcass exulting,

---

[1] For 'néod-laðu' (1321) C. suggests 'néad-láðum,' and translates : *asked whether the night had been pleasant to him after crushing-hostility.*

By cramming discovered.[1] The quarrel she wreaked then,
That last night igone Grendel thou killedst

This horrible
creature came to
avenge Grendel's
death.

15 In grewsomest manner, with grim-holding clutches,
Since too long he had lessened my liege-troop and wasted
My folk-men so foully. He fell in the battle
With forfeit of life, and another has followed,
A mighty crime-worker, her kinsman avenging,
20 And henceforth hath 'stablished her hatred unyielding,[2]
As it well may appear to many a liegeman,
Who mourneth in spirit the treasure-bestower,
Her heavy heart-sorrow ; the hand is now lifeless
Which[3] availed you in every wish that you cherished.

25 Land-people heard I, liegemen, this saying,
Dwellers in halls, they had seen very often

I have heard my
vassals speak of
these two uncanny
monsters who lived
in the moors.

A pair of such mighty march-striding creatures,
Far-dwelling spirits, holding the moorlands :
One of them wore, as well they might notice,
30 The image of woman, the other one wretched
In guise of a man wandered in exile,
Except he was huger than any of earthmen ;
Earth-dwelling people entitled him Grendel
In days of yore : they know not their father,
35 Whe'r ill-going spirits any were borne him
Ever before. They guard the wolf-coverts,

They inhabit the
most desolate and
horrible places.

Lands inaccessible, wind-beaten nesses,
Fearfullest fen-deeps, where a flood from the mountains
'Neath mists of the nesses netherward rattles,
40 The stream under earth : not far is it henceward
Measured by mile-lengths that the mere-water standeth,
Which forests hang over, with frost-whiting covered,[4]

---

[1] For 'gefrægnod' (1334), K. and t. B. suggest 'gefægnod,' rendering
' *rejoicing in her fill.*' This gives a parallel to ' æse wlanc ' (1333).

[2] The line 'And . . . yielding,' B. renders: *And she has performed a deed
of blood-vengeance whose effect is far-reaching.*

[3] 'Sé þe ' (1345) is an instance of masc. rel. with fem. antecedent. So
v. 1888, where 'sé þé ' refers to 'yldo.'

[4] For 'hrímge' in the Il.-So. edition, Gr. and others read ' hrínde '
(= hrínende), and translate : *which rustling forests overhang.*

A firm-rooted forest, the floods overshadow.
There ever at night one an ill-meaning portent
45 A fire-flood may see ; 'mong children of men
None liveth so wise that wot of the bottom ;
Though harassed by hounds the heath-stepper seek for,

Fly to the forest, firm-antlered he-deer,
Spurred from afar, his spirit he yieldeth,
50 His life on the shore, ere in he will venture
To cover his head.   Uncanny the place is :
Thence upward ascendeth the surging of waters,
Wan to the welkin, when the wind is stirring
The weathers unpleasing, till the air groweth gloomy,

55 And the heavens lower.   Now is help to be gotten
From thee and thee only !   The abode thou know'st not,
The dangerous place where thou'rt able to meet with
The sin-laden hero :   seek if thou darest !
For the feud I will fully fee thee with money,
60 With old-time treasure, as erstwhile I did thee,
With well-twisted jewels, if away thou shalt get thee."

XXII.

BEOWULF SEEKS GRENDEL'S MOTHER.

Beowulf answered, Ecgtheow's son :

"Grieve not, O wise one ! for each it is better,
His friend to avenge than with vehemence wail him ;
Each of us must the end-day abide of
5 His earthly existence ; who is able accomplish
Glory ere death !   To battle-thane noble
Lifeless lying, 'tis at last most fitting.
Arise, O king, quick let us hasten
To look at the footprint of the kinsman of Grendel !
10 I promise thee this now : to his place he'll escape not,
To embrace of the earth, nor to mountainous forest,
Nor to depths of the ocean, wherever he wanders.

Practice thou now patient endurance
Of each of thy sorrows, as I hope for thee soothly!"

15 Then up sprang the old one, the All-Wielder thanked he,
Ruler Almighty, that the man had outspoken.
Then for Hrothgar a war-horse was decked with a bridle,
Curly-maned courser. The clever folk-leader
Stately proceeded: stepped then an earl-troop

20 Of linden-wood bearers. Her footprints were seen then
Widely in wood-paths, her way o'er the bottoms,
Where she faraway fared o'er fen-country murky,
Bore away breathless the best of retainers
Who pondered with Hrothgar the welfare of country.

25 The son of the athelings then went o'er the stony,
Declivitous cliffs, the close-covered passes,
Narrow passages, paths unfrequented,
Nesses abrupt, nicker-haunts many;
One of a few of wise-mooded heroes,

30 He onward advanced to view the surroundings,
Till he found unawares woods of the mountain
O'er hoar-stones hanging, holt-wood unjoyful;
The water stood under, welling and gory.
'Twas irksome in spirit to all of the Danemen,

35 Friends of the Scyldings, to many a liegeman
Sad to be suffered, a sorrow unlittle
To each of the earlmen, when to Æschere's head they
Came on the cliff. The current was seething
With blood and with gore (the troopers gazed on it).

40 The horn anon sang the battle-song ready.
The troop were all seated; they saw 'long the water then
Many a serpent, mere-dragons wondrous
Trying the waters, nickers a-lying
On the cliffs of the nesses, which at noonday full often

45 Go on the sea-deeps their sorrowful journey,
Wild-beasts and wormkind; away then they hastened
Hot-mooded, hateful, they heard the great clamor,
The war-trumpet winding. One did the Geat-prince

Hrothgar rouses himself. His horse is brought.

They start on the track of the female monster.

The sight of Æschere's head causes them great sorrow.

The water is filled with serpents and sea-dragons.

One of them is killed by Beowulf.

Sunder from earth-joys, with arrow from bowstring,
50 From his sea-struggle tore him, that the trusty war-missile

The dead beast is a poor swimmer.

Pierced to his vitals ;' he proved in the currents
Less doughty at swimming whom death had offcarried.
Soon in the waters the wonderful swimmer
Was straitened most sorely with sword-pointed boar-spears,
55 Pressed in the battle and pulled to the cliff-edge ;
The liegemen then looked on the loath-fashioned stranger.

Beowulf prepares for a struggle with the fire-drake.

Beowulf donned then his battle-equipments,
Cared little for life ; inlaid and most ample,
The hand-woven corslet which could cover his body,
60 Must the wave-deeps explore, that war might be powerless
To harm the great hero, and the hating one's grasp might
Not peril his safety ; his head was protected
By the light-flashing helmet that should mix with the bot-
      toms,
Trying the eddies, treasure-emblazoned,
65 Encircled with jewels, as in seasons long past
The weapon-smith worked it, wondrously made it,
With swine-bodies fashioned it, that thenceforward no longer
Brand might bite it, and battle-sword hurt it.
And that was not least of helpers in prowess

He has Unferth's sword in his hand.

70 That Hrothgar's spokesman had lent him when straitened ;
And the hilted hand-sword was Hrunting entitled,
Old and most excellent 'mong all of the treasures ;
Its blade was of iron, blotted with poison,
Hardened with gore ; it failed not in battle
75 Any hero under heaven in hand who it brandished,
Who ventured to take the terrible journeys,
The battle-field sought ; not the earliest occasion
That deeds of daring 'twas destined to 'complish.

Unferth has little use for swords.

Ecglaf's kinsman minded not soothly,
80 Exulting in strength, what erst he had spoken
Drunken with wine, when the weapon he lent to
A sword-hero bolder ; himself did not venture
'Neath the strife of the currents his life to endanger,

To fame-deeds perform ; there he forfeited glory,
85 Repute for his strength.   Not so with the other
When he clad in his corslet had equipped him for battle.

XXIII.

BEOWULF'S FIGHT WITH GRENDEL'S MOTHER.

Beowulf spake, Ecgtheow's son :

    Beowulf makes a parting speech to Hrothgar.

" Recall now, oh, famous kinsman of Healfdene,
Prince very prudent, now to part I am ready,
Gold-friend of earlmen, what erst we agreed on,
5 Should I lay down my life in lending thee assistance,

    If I fall, act as a kind liegelord to my thanes,

When my earth-joys were over, thou wouldst evermore serve me
In stead of a father ; my faithful thanemen,
My trusty retainers, protect thou and care for,
Fall I in battle : and, Hrothgar belovèd,
10 Send unto Higelac the high-valued jewels

    and send Higelac the jewels thou hast given me.

Thou to me hast allotted.   The lord of the Geatmen
May perceive from the gold, the Hrethling may see it
When he looks on the jewels, that a gem-giver found I
Good over-measure, enjoyed him while able.

    I should like my king to know how generous a lord I found thee to be.

15 And the ancient heirloom Unferth permit thou,
The famed one to have, the heavy-sword splendid[1]
The hard-edgèd weapon ; with Hrunting to aid me,
I shall gain me glory, or grim-death shall take me."
The atheling of Geatmen uttered these words and

    Beowulf is eager for the fray.

20 Heroic did hasten, not any rejoinder
Was willing to wait for ; the wave-current swallowed
The doughty-in-battle.   Then a day's-length elapsed ere

    He is a whole day reaching the bottom of the sea.

He was able to see the sea at its bottom.
Early she found then who fifty of winters
25 The course of the currents kept in her fury,
Grisly and greedy, that the grim one's dominion

---

[1] Kl. emends ' wæl-sweord.'   The half-line would then read, ' *the battle-sword splendid.*' — For ' heard-ecg ' in next half-verse, see note to 20₃₉ above.

Grendel's mother
knows that some
one has reached
her domains.

Some one of men from above was exploring.

Forth did she grab them, grappled the warrior

With horrible clutches; yet no sooner she injured

30 His body unscathèd: the burnie out-guarded,

That she proved but powerless to pierce through the armor,

The limb-mail locked, with loath-grabbing fingers.

The sea-wolf bare then, when bottomward came she,

She grabs him,
and bears him to
her den.

The ring-prince homeward, that he after was powerless

35 (He had daring to do it) to deal with his weapons,

But many a mere-beast tormented him swimming,

Sea-monsters bite
and strike him.

Flood-beasts no few with fierce-biting tusks did

Break through his burnie, the brave one pursued they.

The earl then discovered he was down in some cavern

40 Where no water whatever anywise harmed him,

And the clutch of the current could come not anear him,

Since the roofed-hall prevented; brightness a-gleaming

Fire-light he saw, flashing resplendent.

The good one saw then the sea-bottom's monster,

Beowulf attacks
the mother of
Grendel.

45 The mighty mere-woman; he made a great onset

With weapon-of-battle, his hand not desisted

From striking, that war-blade struck on her head then

A battle-song greedy. The stranger perceived then

The sword will not
bite.

The sword would not bite, her life would not injure,

50 But the falchion failed the folk-prince when straitened:

Erst had it often onsets encountered,

Oft cloven the helmet, the fated one's armor:

'Twas the first time that ever the excellent jewel

Had failed of its fame. Firm-mooded after,

55 Not heedless of valor, but mindful of glory,

Was Higelac's kinsman; the hero-chief angry

Cast then his carved-sword covered with jewels

That it lay on the earth, hard and steel-pointed;

The hero throws
down all weapons,
and again trusts
to his hand-grip.

He hoped in his strength, his hand-grapple sturdy.

60 So any must act whenever he thinketh

To gain him in battle glory unending,

And is reckless of living. The lord of the War-Geats

(He shrank not from battle) seized by the shoulder [1]
The mother of Grendel ; then mighty in struggle
65 Swung he his enemy, since his anger was kindled,
That she fell to the floor.   With furious grapple
She gave him requital [2] early thereafter,
And stretched out to grab him ; the strongest of warriors
Faint-mooded stumbled, till he fell in his traces,
70 Foot-going champion.   Then she sat on the hall-guest
And wielded her war-knife wide-bladed, flashing,
For her son would take vengeance, her one only bairn.
His breast-armor woven bode on his shoulder ;
It guarded his life, the entrance defended
75 'Gainst sword-point and edges.   Ecgtheow's son there
Had fatally journeyed, champion of Geatmen,
In the arms of the ocean, had the armor not given,
Close-woven corslet, comfort and succor,
And had God most holy not awarded the victory,
80 All-knowing Lord ; easily did heaven's
Ruler most righteous arrange it with justice ; [3]
Uprose he erect ready for battle.

Beowulf falls.

The monster sits on him with drawn sword.

His armor saves his life.

God arranged for his escape.

XXIV.

BEOWULF IS DOUBLE-CONQUEROR.

Then he saw mid the war-gems a weapon of victory,
An ancient giant-sword, of edges a-doughty,
Glory of warriors : of weapons 'twas choicest,
Only 'twas larger than any man else was

Beowulf grasps a giant-sword,

---

[1] Sw., R., and t. B. suggest ' feaxe ' for ' eaxle ' (1538) and render: *Seized by the hair.*

[2] If ' hand-léan ' be accepted (as the MS. has it), the line will read : *She hand-reward gave him early thereafter.*

[3] Sw. and S. change H.-So.'s semicolon (v. 1557) to a comma, and translate: *The Ruler of Heaven arranged it in justice easily, after he arose again.*

    5 Able to bear to the battle-encounter,
        The good and splendid work of the giants.
        He grasped then the sword-hilt, knight of the Scyldings,
        Bold and battle-grim, brandished his ring-sword,
        Hopeless of living, hotly he smote her,

and fells the female monster.
    10 That the fiend-woman's neck firmly it grappled,
        Broke through her bone-joints, the bill fully pierced her
        Fate-cursèd body, she fell to the ground then:
        The hand-sword was bloody, the hero exulted.
        The brand was brilliant, brightly it glimmered,

    15 Just as from heaven gemlike shineth
        The torch of the firmament. He glanced 'long the building,
        And turned by the wall then, Higelac's vassal
        Raging and wrathful raised his battle-sword
        Strong by the handle. The edge was not useless

    20 To the hero-in-battle, but he speedily wished to
        Give Grendel requital for the many assaults he
        Had worked on the West-Danes not once, but often,
        When he slew in slumber the subjects of Hrothgar,
        Swallowed down fifteen sleeping retainers

    25 Of the folk of the Danemen, and fully as many
        Carried away, a horrible prey.
        He gave him requital, grim-raging champion,

Beowulf sees the body of Grendel, and cuts off his head.
        When he saw on his rest-place weary of conflict
        Grendel lying, of life-joys bereavèd,

    30 As the battle at Heorot erstwhile had scathed him;
        His body far bounded, a blow when he suffered,
        Death having seized him, sword-smiting heavy,
        And he cut off his head then. Early this noticed
        The clever carles who as comrades of Hrothgar

The waters are gory.
    35 Gazed on the sea-deeps, that the surging wave-currents
        Were mightily mingled, the mere-flood was gory:
        Of the good one the gray-haired together held converse,

Beowulf is given up for dead.
        The hoary of head, that they hoped not to see again
        The atheling ever, that exulting in victory

    40 He'd return there to visit the distinguished folk-ruler:

Then many concluded the mere-wolf had killed him.[1]
The ninth hour came then.   From the ness-edge departed
The bold-mooded Scyldings ; the gold-friend of heroes
Homeward betook him.   The strangers sat down then
45 Soul-sick, sorrowful, the sea-waves regarding :
They wished and yet weened not their well-loved friend-lord
To see any more.   The sword-blade began then,
The blood having touched it, contracting and shriveling
With battle-icicles ; 'twas a wonderful marvel
50 That it melted entirely, likest to ice when
The Father unbindeth the bond of the frost and
Unwindeth the wave-bands, He who wieldeth dominion
Of times and of tides : a truth-firm Creator.
Nor took he of jewels more in the dwelling,
55 Lord of the Weders, though they lay all around him,
Than the head and the handle handsome with jewels ;

The giant-sword melts.

---

[1] ' þæs monige gewearð ' (1599) and ' hafað þæs geworden ' (2027). — In a
paper published some years ago in one of the Johns Hopkins University
circulars, I tried to throw upon these two long-doubtful passages some light
derived from a study of like passages in Alfred's prose. — The impersonal verb
'geweorðan,' with an accus. of the person, and a þæt-clause is used several
times with the meaning 'agree.' See Orosius (Sweet's ed.) 178₇; 204₃₁;
208₂₈; 210₁₅; 280₂₀. In the two Beowulf passages, the þæt-clause is antici-
pated by ' þæs,' which is clearly a gen. of the thing agreed on.

The first passage (v. 1599 (b)–1600) I translate literally : *Then many
agreed upon this (namely), that the sea-wolf had killed him.*

The second passage (v. 2025 (b)–2027): *She is promised . . . ; to this the
friend of the Scyldings has agreed, etc.* By emending 'is' instead of 'was'
(2025), the tenses will be brought into perfect harmony.

In v. 1997 ff. this same idiom occurs, and was noticed in B.'s great
article on Beowulf, which appeared about the time I published my reading
of 1599 and 2027. Translate 1997 then: *Wouldst let the South-Danes themselves decide about their struggle with Grendel.* Here 'Súð-Dene' is accus.
of person, and 'gúðe' is gen. of thing agreed on.

With such collateral support as that afforded by B. (P. and B. XII. 97), I
have no hesitation in departing from H.-So., my usual guide. — The idiom above treated runs through A.-S., Old Saxon, and other Teutonic
languages, and should be noticed in the lexicons.

The brand early melted, burnt was the weapon :[1]
So hot was the blood, the strange-spirit poisonous

The hero swims
back to the realms
of day.
That in it did perish.   He early swam off then
60 Who had bided in combat the carnage of haters,
Went up through the ocean ; the eddies were cleansèd,
The spacious expanses, when the spirit from farland
His life put aside and this short-lived existence.
The seamen's defender came swimming to land then
65 Doughty of spirit, rejoiced in his sea-gift,
The bulky burden which he bore in his keeping.
The excellent vassals advanced then to meet him,
To God they were grateful, were glad in their chieftain,
That to see him safe and sound was granted them.
70 From the high-minded hero, then, helmet and burnie
Were speedily loosened : the ocean was putrid,
The water 'neath welkin weltered with gore.
Forth did they fare, then, their footsteps retracing,
Merry and mirthful, measured the earth-way,
75 The highway familiar : men very daring[2]
Bare then the head from the sea-cliff, burdening
Each of the earlmen, excellent-valiant.

It takes four men
to carry Grendel's
head on a spear.
Four of them had to carry with labor
The head of Grendel to the high towering gold-hall
80 Upstuck on the spear, till fourteen most-valiant
And battle-brave Geatmen came there going
Straight to the palace : the prince of the people
Measured the mead-ways, their mood-brave companion.
The atheling of earlmen entered the building,
85 Deed-valiant man, adorned with distinction,
Doughty shield-warrior, to address King Hrothgar :

---

[1] 'Bróden-mæl' is regarded by most scholars as meaning a damaskeened
sword.   Translate : *The damaskeened sword burned up.* Cf. 25_{16} and note.

[2] 'Cyning-balde' (1635) is the much-disputed reading of K. and Th.   To
render this, " *nobly bold*," " *excellently bold*," have been suggested.   B. would
read 'cyning-holde' (cf. 290), and render : *Men well-disposed towards the
king carried the head, etc.* 'Cynebealde,' says t. B., endorsing Gr.

Then hung by the hair, the head of Grendel
Was borne to the building, where beer-thanes were drinking,
Loth before earlmen and eke 'fore the lady :
90 The warriors beheld then a wonderful sight.

XXV.

BEOWULF BRINGS HIS TROPHIES.—HROTHGAR'S GRATITUDE.

Beowulf spake, offspring of Ecgtheow :   Beowulf relates his
                                                           last exploit.
" Lo ! we blithely have brought thee, bairn of Healfdene,
Prince of the Scyldings, these presents from ocean
Which thine eye looketh on, for an emblem of glory.
5 I came off alive from this, narrowly 'scaping :
In war 'neath the water the work with great pains I
Performed, and the fight had been finished quite nearly,
Had God not defended me.   I failed in the battle
Aught to accomplish, aided by Hrunting,
10 Though that weapon was worthy, but the Wielder of earth-folk
Gave me willingly to see on the wall a   God was fighting
                                                           with me.
Heavy old hand-sword hanging in splendor
(He guided most often the lorn and the friendless),
That I swung as a weapon.   The wards of the house then
15 I killed in the conflict (when occasion was given me).
Then the battle-sword burned, the brand that was lifted,[1]
As the blood-current sprang, hottest of war-sweats ;
Seizing the hilt, from my foes I offbore it ;
I avenged as I ought to their acts of malignity,
20 The murder of Danemen.   I then make thee this promise,   Heorot is freed
Thou'lt be able in Heorot careless to slumber   from monsters.
With thy throng of heroes and the thanes of thy people
Every and each, of greater and lesser,
And thou needest not fear for them from the selfsame direction
25 As thou formerly fearedst, oh, folk-lord of Scyldings,

---

[1] Or rather, perhaps, '*the inlaid, or damaskeened weapon.*' Cf. 24₅₇ and note.

End-day for earlmen." To the age-hoary man then,

The gray-haired chieftain, the gold-fashioned sword-hilt,
Old-work of giants, was thereupon given ;
Since the fall of the fiends, it fell to the keeping
30 Of the wielder of Danemen, the wonder-smith's labor,
And the bad-mooded being abandoned this world then,
Opponent of God, victim of murder,
And also his mother ; it went to the keeping
Of the best of the world-kings, where waters encircle,
35 Who the scot divided in Scylding dominion.

Hrothgar discoursed, the hilt he regarded,
The ancient heirloom where an old-time contention's
Beginning was graven : the gurgling currents,
The flood slew thereafter the race of the giants,
40 They had proved themselves daring : that people was loth to

The Lord everlasting, through lash of the billows
The Father gave them final requital.
So in letters of rune on the clasp of the handle
Gleaming and golden, 'twas graven exactly,
45 Set forth and said, whom that sword had been made for,
Finest of irons, who first it was wrought for,
Wreathed at its handle and gleaming with serpents.
The wise one then said (silent they all were)

Son of old Healfdene : " He may say unrefuted
50 Who performs 'mid the folk-men fairness and truth
(The hoary old ruler remembers the past),
That better by birth is this bairn of the nobles !
Thy fame is extended through far-away countries,
Good friend Beowulf, o'er all of the races,
55 Thou holdest all firmly, hero-like strength with
Prudence of spirit. I'll prove myself grateful
As before we agreed on ; thou granted for long shalt
Become a great comfort to kinsmen and comrades,

A help unto heroes. Heremod became not
60 Such to the Scyldings, successors of Ecgwela ;
He grew not to please them, but grievous destruction,

And diresome death-woes to Danemen attracted ;
He slew in anger his table-companions,
Trustworthy counsellors, till he turned off lonely
65 From world-joys away, wide-famous ruler :
Though high-ruling heaven in hero-strength raised him,
In might exalted him, o'er men of all nations
Made him supreme, yet a murderous spirit
Grew in his bosom : he gave then no ring-gems
70 To the Danes after custom ; endured he unjoyful
Standing the straits from strife that was raging,
Longsome folk-sorrow.   Learn then from this,
Lay hold of virtue !   Though laden with winters,
I have sung thee these measures.   'Tis a marvel to tell it,
75 How all-ruling God from greatness of spirit
Giveth wisdom to children of men,
Manor and earlship : all things He ruleth.
He often permitteth the mood-thought of man of
The illustrious' lineage to lean to possessions,
80 Allows him earthly delights at his manor,
A high-burg of heroes to hold in his keeping,
Maketh portions of earth-folk hear him,
And a wide-reaching kingdom so that, wisdom failing him,
He himself is unable to reckon its boundaries ;
85 He liveth in luxury, little debars him,
Nor sickness nor age, no treachery-sorrow
Becloudeth his spirit, conflict nowhere,
No sword-hate, appeareth, but all of the world doth
Wend as he wisheth ; the worse he knoweth not,
90 Till arrant arrogance inward pervading,
Waxeth and springeth, when the warder is sleeping,
The guard of the soul : with sorrows encompassed,
Too sound is his slumber, the slayer is near him,
Who with bow and arrow aimeth in malice.

A wretched failure of a king, to give no jewels to his retainers.

Hrothgar moralizes.

XXVI.

HROTHGAR MORALIZES.— REST AFTER LABOR.

A wounded spirit.

" Then bruised in his bosom he with bitter-toothed missile
Is hurt 'neath his helmet : from harmful pollution
He is powerless to shield him by the wonderful mandates
Of the loath-cursèd spirit ; what too long he hath holden
5 Him seemeth too small, savage he hoardeth,
Nor boastfully giveth gold-plated rings,[1]
The fate of the future flouts and forgetteth
Since God had erst given him greatness no little,
Wielder of Glory.   His end-day anear,
10 It afterward happens that the bodily-dwelling
Fleetingly fadeth, falls into ruins ;
Another lays hold who doleth the ornaments,
The nobleman's jewels, nothing lamenting,
Heedeth no terror.   Oh, Beowulf dear,
15 Best of the heroes, from bale-strife defend thee,
And choose thee the better, counsels eternal ;

Be not over proud: life is fleeting, and its strength soon wasteth away.

Beware of arrogance, world-famous champion !
But a little-while lasts thy life-vigor's fulness ;
'Twill after hap early, that illness or sword-edge
20 Shall part thee from strength, or the grasp of the fire,
Or the wave of the current, or clutch of the edges,
Or flight of the war-spear, or age with its horrors,
Or thine eyes' bright flashing shall fade into darkness :
'Twill happen full early, excellent hero,

Hrothgar gives an account of his reign.

25 That death shall subdue thee.   So the Danes a half-century
I held under heaven, helped them in struggles
'Gainst many a race in middle-earth's regions,
With ash-wood and edges, that enemies none
On earth molested me.   Lo ! offsetting change, now,

---

[1] K. says '*proudly giveth.*' — Gr. says, '*And gives no gold-plated rings, in order to incite the recipient to boastfulness.*' — B. suggests 'gyld' for 'gylp,' and renders: *And gives no beaten rings for reward.*

Sorrow after joy.

30 Came to my manor, grief after joyance,
   When Grendel became my constant visitor,
   Inveterate hater : I from that malice
   Continually travailed with trouble no little.
   Thanks be to God that I gained in my lifetime,
35 To the Lord everlasting, to look on the gory
   Head with mine eyes, after long-lasting sorrow !
   Go to the bench now, battle-adornèd
   Joy in the feasting : of jewels in common
   We'll meet with many when morning appeareth."
40 The Geatman was gladsome, ganged he immediately
   To go to the bench, as the clever one bade him.
   Then again as before were the famous-for-prowess,
   Hall-inhabiters, handsomely banqueted,
   Feasted anew. The night-veil fell then
45 Dark o'er the warriors. The courtiers rose then ;
   The gray-haired was anxious to go to his slumbers,
   The hoary old Scylding. Hankered the Geatman,
   The champion doughty, greatly, to rest him :
   An earlman early outward did lead him,

Beowulf is fagged,
and seeks rest.

50 Fagged from his faring, from far-country springing,
   Who for etiquette's sake all of a liegeman's
   Needs regarded, such as seamen at that time
   Were bounden to feel. The big-hearted rested ;
   The building uptowered, spacious and gilded,
55 The guest within slumbered, till the sable-clad raven
   Blithely foreboded the beacon of heaven.
   Then the bright-shining sun o'er the bottoms came going ;[1]
   The warriors hastened, the heads of the peoples
   Were ready to go again to their peoples,
60 The high-mooded farer would faraway thenceward
   Look for his vessel. The valiant one bade then,[2]

The Geats prepare
to leave Dane-land.

[1] If S.'s emendation be accepted, v. 57 will read: *Then came the light, going bright after darkness : the warriors, etc.*

[2] As the passage stands in H.-So., Unferth presents Beowulf with the sword Hrunting, and B. thanks him for the gift. If, however, the suggestions of Grdtvg.

Offspring of Ecglaf, off to bear Hrunting,
To take his weapon, his well-beloved iron ;
He him thanked for the gift, saying good he accounted
65 The war-friend and mighty, nor chid he with words then
The blade of the brand : 'twas a brave-mooded hero.
When the warriors were ready, arrayed in their trappings,
The atheling dear to the Danemen advanced then
On to the dais, where the other was sitting,
70 Grim-mooded hero, greeted King Hrothgar.

XXVII.

SORROW AT PARTING.

Beowulf spake, Ecgtheow's offspring :
" We men of the water wish to declare now
Fared from far-lands, we're firmly determined
To seek King Higelac. Here have we fitly
5 Been welcomed and feasted, as heart would desire it ;
Good was the greeting. If greater affection
I am anywise able ever on earth to
Gain at thy hands, ruler of heroes,
Than yet I have done, I shall quickly be ready

10 For combat and conflict. O'er the course of the waters
Learn I that neighbors alarm thee with terror,
As haters did whilom, I hither will bring thee
For help unto heroes henchmen by thousands.

I know as to Higelac, the lord of the Geatmen,
15 Though young in years, he yet will permit me,
By words and by works, ward of the people,
Fully to furnish thee forces and bear thee
My lance to relieve thee, if liegemen shall fail thee,
And help of my hand-strength ; if Hrethric be treating,

and M. be accepted, the passage will read : *Then the brave one* (i.e. *Beowulf*)
commanded that Hrunting be borne to the son of Ecglaf (*Unferth*), *bade him
take his sword, his dear weapon ; he* (*B.*) *thanked him* (*U.*) *for the loan, etc.*

20 Bairn of the king, at the court of the Geatmen,
He thereat may find him friends in abundance :
Faraway countries he were better to seek for
Who trusts in himself." Hrothgar discoursed then,
Making rejoinder : "These words thou hast uttered
25 All-knowing God hath given thy spirit !
Ne'er heard I an earlman thus early in life

O Beowulf, thou art wise beyond thy years.

More clever in speaking : thou'rt cautious of spirit,
Mighty of muscle, in mouth-answers prudent.
I count on the hope that, happen it ever
30 That missile shall rob thee of Hrethel's descendant,
Edge-horrid battle, and illness or weapon
Deprive thee of prince, of people's protector,
And life thou yet holdest, the Sea-Geats will never
Find a more fitting folk-lord to choose them,

Should Higelac die, the Geats could find no better successor than thou wouldst make.

35 Gem-ward of heroes, than *thou* mightest prove thee,
If the kingdom of kinsmen thou carest to govern.
Thy mood-spirit likes me the longer the better,
Beowulf dear : thou hast brought it to pass that
To both these peoples peace shall be common,
40 To Geat-folk and Danemen, the strife be suspended,
The secret assailings they suffered in yore-days ;

Thou hast healed the ancient breach between our races.

And also that jewels be shared while I govern
The wide-stretching kingdom, and that many shall visit
Others o'er the ocean with excellent gift-gems :
45 The ring-adorned bark shall bring o'er the currents
Presents and love-gifts. This people I know
Tow'rd foeman and friend firmly established,[1]
After ancient etiquette everywise blameless."
Then the warden of earlmen gave him still farther,
50 Kinsman of Healfdene, a dozen of jewels,

Parting gifts.

Bade him safely seek with the presents
His well-beloved people, early returning.

[1] For 'geworhte,' the crux of this passage, B. proposes 'geþóhte,' rendering :
I know this people with firm thought every way blameless towards foe and friends.

Hrothgar kisses
Beowulf, and
weeps.

Then the noble-born king kissed the distinguished,
Dear-lovèd liegeman, the Dane-prince saluted him,
55　And claspèd his neck ; tears from him fell,
From the gray-headed man : he two things expected,
Agèd and reverend, but rather the second,
[1] That bold in council they'd meet thereafter.
The man was so dear that he failed to suppress the
60　Emotions that moved him, but in mood-fetters fastened

The old king is
deeply grieved to
part with his bene-
factor.

The long-famous hero longeth in secret
Deep in his spirit for the dear-beloved man
Though not a blood-kinsman.　Beowulf thenceward,
Gold-splendid warrior, walked o'er the meadows
65　Exulting in treasure : the sea-going vessel
Riding at anchor awaited its owner.
As they pressed on their way then, the present of Hrothgar

Giving liberally is
the true proof of
kingship.

Was frequently referred to : a folk-king indeed that
Everyway blameless, till age did debar him
70　The joys of his might, which hath many oft-injured.

XXVIII.

THE HOMEWARD JOURNEY.—THE TWO QUEENS.

Then the band of very valiant retainers
Came to the current ; they were clad all in armor,

The coast-guard
again.

In link-woven burnies.　The land-warder noticed
The return of the earlmen, as he erstwhile had seen them ;
5　Nowise with insult he greeted the strangers
From the naze of the cliff, but rode on to meet them ;
Said the bright-armored visitors [2] vesselward traveled

---

[1] S. and B. emend so as to negative the verb 'meet.' "Why should
Hrothgar weep if he expects to meet Beowulf again?" both these scholars
ask.　But the weeping is mentioned before the 'expectations': the tears may
have been due to many emotions, especially gratitude, struggling for expression.

[2] For 'scawan' (1896), 'scaðan' has been proposed.　Accepting this, we
may render : *He said the bright-armored warriors were going to their vessel,
welcome, etc.*　(Cf. 1804.)

Welcome to Weders. The wide-bosomed craft then
Lay on the sand, laden with armor,
10 With horses and jewels, the ring-stemmèd sailer :
The mast uptowered o'er the treasure of Hrothgar.
To the boat-ward a gold-bound brand he presented,
That he was afterwards honored on the ale-bench more highly
As the heirloom's owner. [1] Set he out on his vessel,
15 To drive on the deep, Dane-country left he.
Along by the mast then a sea-garment fluttered,
A rope-fastened sail. The sea-boat resounded,
The wind o'er the waters the wave-floater nowise
Kept from its journey ; the sea-goer traveled,
20 The foamy-necked floated forth o'er the currents,
The well-fashioned vessel o'er the ways of the ocean,
Till they came within sight of the cliffs of the Geatmen,
The well-known headlands. The wave-goer hastened
Driven by breezes, stood on the shore.   .
25 Prompt at the ocean, the port-ward was ready,
Who long in the past outlooked in the distance,[2]
At water's-edge waiting well-lovèd heroes ;
He bound to the bank then the broad-bosomed vessel
Fast in its fetters, lest the force of the waters
30 Should be able to injure the ocean-wood winsome.
Bade he up then take the treasure of princes,
Plate-gold and fretwork ; not far was it thence
To go off in search of the giver of jewels :

Beowulf gives the guard a handsome sword.

The Geats see their own land again.

The port-warden is anxiously looking for them.

---

[1] R. suggests, 'Gewát him on naca,' and renders: *The vessel set out, to drive on the sea, the Dane-country left.* 'On' bears the alliteration; cf. 'on hafu' (2524). This has some advantages over the H.-So. reading; viz. (1) It adds nothing to the text; (2) it makes 'naca' the subject, and thus brings the passage into keeping with the context, where the poet has exhausted his vocabulary in detailing the actions of the vessel. — B.'s emendation (cf. P. and B. XII. 97) is violent.

[2] B. translates: *Who for a long time, ready at the coast, had looked out into the distance eagerly for the dear men.* This changes the syntax of 'léofra manna.'

Hrethel's son Higelac at home there remaineth,[1]
35 Himself with his comrades close to the sea-coast.
The building was splendid, the king heroic,
Great in his hall, Hygd very young was,

Hygd, the noble queen of Higelac, lavish of gifts.

Fine-mooded, clever, though few were the winters
That the daughter of Hæreth had dwelt in the borough ;
40 But she nowise was cringing nor niggard of presents,
Of ornaments rare, to the race of the Geatmen.

Offa's consort, Thrytho, is contrasted with Hygd.

Thrytho nursed anger, excellent[2] folk-queen,
Hot-burning hatred : no hero whatever
'Mong household companions, her husband excepted,

She is a terror to all save her husband.

45 Dared to adventure to look at the woman
With eyes in the daytime ;[3] but he knew that death-chains
Hand-wreathed were wrought him : early thereafter,
When the hand-strife was over, edges were ready,
That fierce-raging sword-point had to force a decision,
50 Murder-bale show.   Such no womanly custom
For a lady to practise, though lovely her person,
That a weaver-of-peace, on pretence of anger
A belovèd liegeman of life should deprive.
Soothly this hindered Heming's kinsman ;
55 Other ale-drinking earlmen asserted
That fearful folk-sorrows fewer she wrought them,
Treacherous doings, since first she was given
Adornèd with gold to the war-hero youthful,
For her origin honored, when Offa's great palace
60 O'er the fallow flood by her father's instructions
She sought on her journey, where she afterwards fully,
Famed for her virtue, her fate on the king's-seat

---

[1] For 'wunað' (v. 1924) several eminent critics suggest 'wunade' (= remained).   This makes the passage much clearer.

[2] Why should such a woman be described as an 'excellent' queen? C. suggests 'frécnu' = dangerous, bold.

[3] For 'an dæges' various readings have been offered. If 'and-éges' be accepted, the sentence will read: *No hero . . . dared look upon her, eye to eye.* If 'án-dæges' be adopted, translate: *Dared look upon her the whole day.*

Enjoyed in her lifetime, love did she hold with
The ruler of heroes, the best, it is told me,
65 Of all of the earthmen that oceans encompass,
Of earl-kindreds endless; hence Offa was famous
Far and widely, by gifts and by battles,
Spear-valiant hero; the home of his fathers
He governed with wisdom, whence Eomær did issue
70 For help unto heroes, Heming's kinsman,
Grandson of Garmund, great in encounters.

XXIX.

BEOWULF AND HIGELAC.

Then the brave one departed, his band along with him,
Seeking the sea-shore, the sea-marches treading,

Beowulf and his
party seek Higelac.

The wide-stretching shores. The world-candle glimmered,
The sun from the southward; they proceeded then onward,
5 Early arriving where they heard that the troop-lord,
Ongentheow's slayer, excellent, youthful
Folk-prince and warrior was distributing jewels,
Close in his castle. The coming of Beowulf
Was announced in a message quickly to Higelac,
10 That the folk-troop's defender forth to the palace
The linden-companion alive was advancing,
Secure from the combat courtward a-going.
The building was early inward made ready
For the foot-going guests as the good one had ordered.
15 He sat by the man then who had lived through the struggle,

Beowulf sits by his
liegelord.

Kinsman by kinsman, when the king of the people
Had in lordly language saluted the dear one,
In words that were formal. The daughter of Hæreth

Queen Hygd re-
ceives the heroes,

Coursed through the building, carrying mead-cups : [1]

---

[1] 'Meodu-scencum' (1981) some would render '*with mead-pourers.*' Translate then : *The daughter of Hæreth went through the building accompanied by
mead-pourers.*

20 She loved the retainers, tendered the beakers
    To the high-minded Geatmen.   Higelac 'gan then

Higelac is greatly
interested in Beo-
wulf's adventures.

    Pleasantly plying his companion with questions
    In the high-towering palace.   A curious interest
    Tormented his spirit, what meaning to see in
25 The Sea-Geats' adventures : " Beowulf worthy,

Give an account of
thy adventures,
Beowulf dear.

    How throve your journeying, when thou thoughtest suddenly
    Far o'er the salt-streams to seek an encounter,
    A battle at Heorot?   Hast bettered for Hrothgar,
    The famous folk-leader, his far-published sorrows
30 Any at all?   In agony-billows

My suspense has
been great.

    I mused upon torture, distrusted the journey
    Of the belovèd liegeman ; I long time did pray thee
    By no means to seek out the murderous spirit,
    To suffer the South-Danes themselves to decide on [1]
35 Grappling with Grendel.   To God I am thankful
    To be suffered to see thee safe from thy journey."

Beowulf narrates
his adventures.

    Beowulf answered, bairn of old Ecgtheow :
    " 'Tis hidden by no means, Higelac chieftain,
    From many of men, the meeting so famous,
40 What mournful moments of me and of Grendel
    Were passed in the place where he pressing affliction
    On the Victory-Scyldings scathefully brought,
    Anguish forever ; that all I avengèd,
    So that any under heaven of the kinsmen of Grendel

Grendel's kindred
have no cause to
boast.

45 Needeth not boast of that cry-in-the-morning,
    Who longest liveth of the loth-going kindred,[2]
    Encompassed by moorland.   I came in my journey
    To the royal ring-hall, Hrothgar to greet there :

Hrothgar received
me very cordially.

    Soon did the famous scion of Healfdene,
50 When he understood fully the spirit that led me,
    Assign me a seat with the son of his bosom.

---

[1] See my note to 1599, supra, and B. in P. and B. XII. 97.
[2] For 'fenne,' supplied by Grdtvg., B. suggests 'fácne' (cf. Jul. 350).
Accepting this, translate : *Who longest lives of the hated race, steeped in
treachery.*

The troop was in joyance; mead-glee greater
'Neath arch of the ether not ever beheld I
'Mid hall-building holders. The highly-famed queen,

55 Peace-tie of peoples, oft passed through the building,
Cheered the young troopers; she oft tendered a hero
A beautiful ring-band, ere she went to her sitting.
Oft the daughter of Hrothgar in view of the courtiers
To the earls at the end the ale-vessel carried,

60 Whom Freaware I heard then hall-sitters title,
When nail-adorned jewels she gave to the heroes:
Gold-bedecked, youthful, to the glad son of Froda
Her faith has been plighted; the friend of the Scyldings,
The guard of the kingdom, hath given his sanction,[1]

65 And counts it a vantage, for a part of the quarrels,
A portion of hatred, to pay with the woman.
[2] Somewhere not rarely, when the ruler has fallen,
The life-taking lance relaxeth its fury
For a brief breathing-spell, though the bride be charming!

The queen also showed us no little honor.

Hrothgar's lovely daughter.

She is betrothed to Ingeld, in order to unite the Danes and Heathobards.

XXX.

BEOWULF NARRATES HIS ADVENTURES TO HIGELAC.

" It well may discomfit the prince of the Heathobards
And each of the thanemen of earls that attend him,

[1] See note to v. 1599 above.

[2] This is perhaps the least understood sentence in the poem, almost every word being open to dispute. (1) The 'nó' of our text is an emendation, and is rejected by many scholars. (2) 'Seldan' is by some taken as an adv. (= *seldom*), and by others as a noun (= *page, companion*). (3) 'Léod-hryre,' some render '*fall of the people*'; others, '*fall of the prince.*' (4) 'Bûgeð,' most scholars regard as the intrans. verb meaning '*bend*,' '*rest*'; but one great scholar has translated it '*shall kill.*' (5) 'Hwær,' very recently, has been attacked, 'wære' being suggested. (6) As a corollary to the above, the same critic proposes to drop 'oft' out of the text. — t. B. suggests: Oft seldan wære after léodhryre: lytle hwíle bongár bûgeð, þeah séo brýd duge = *often has a treaty been (thus) struck, after a prince had fallen: (but only) a short time is the spear (then) wont to rest, however excellent the bride may be.*

When he goes to the building escorting the woman,
That a noble-born Daneman the knights should be feasting :
5 There gleam on his person the leavings of elders
Hard and ring-bright, Heathobards' treasure,
While they wielded their arms, till they misled to the battle
Their own dear lives and belovèd companions.
He saith at the banquet who the collar beholdeth,
10 An ancient ash-warrior who earlmen's destruction
Clearly recalleth (cruel his spirit),
Sadly beginneth sounding the youthful
Thane-champion's spirit through the thoughts of his bosom,
War-grief to waken, and this word-answer speaketh :

Ingeld is stirred up
to break the truce. 15 'Art thou able, my friend, to know when thou seest it
The brand which thy father bare to the conflict
In his latest adventure, 'neath visor of helmet,
The dearly-loved iron, where Danemen did slay him,
And brave-mooded Scyldings, on the fall of the heroes,
20 (When vengeance was sleeping) the slaughter-place wielded?
E'en now some man of the murderer's progeny
Exulting in ornaments enters the building,
Boasts of his blood-shedding, offbeareth the jewel
Which thou shouldst wholly hold in possession !'
25 So he urgeth and mindeth on every occasion
With woe-bringing words, till waxeth the season
When the woman's thane for the works of his father,
The bill having bitten, blood-gory sleepeth,
Fated to perish ; the other one thenceward
30 'Scapeth alive, the land knoweth thoroughly.[1]
Then the oaths of the earlmen on each side are broken,
When rancors unresting are raging in Ingeld
And his wife-love waxeth less warm after sorrow.
So the Heathobards' favor not faithful I reckon,
35 Their part in the treaty not true to the Danemen,
Their friendship not fast.   I further shall tell thee

---

[1] For 'lifigende' (2063), a mere conjecture, 'wigende' has been suggested.
The line would then read : *Escapeth by fighting, knows the land thoroughly.*

More about Grendel, that thou fully mayst hear,
Ornament-giver, what afterward came from
The hand-rush of heroes. When the jewel of heaven
40 O'er earthfields had gilded, the stranger came raging,
The horrible night-fiend, us for to visit,
Where wholly unharmed the hall we were guarding.
To Hondscio happened a hopeless contention,
Death to the doomed one, dead he fell foremost,
45 Girded war-champion; to him Grendel became then,
To the vassal distinguished, a tooth-weaponed murderer,
The well-beloved henchman's body all swallowed.
Not the earlier off empty of hand did
The bloody-toothed murderer, mindful of evils,
50 Wish to escape from the gold-giver's palace,
But sturdy of strength he strove to outdo me,
Hand-ready grappled. A glove was suspended
Spacious and wondrous, in art-fetters fastened,
Which was fashioned entirely by touch of the craftman
55 From the dragon's skin by the devil's devices:
He down in its depths would do me unsadly
One among many, deed-doer raging,
Though sinless he saw me; not so could it happen
When I in my anger upright did stand.
60 'Tis too long to recount how requital I furnished
For every evil to the earlmen's destroyer;
'Twas there, my prince, that I proudly distinguished
Thy land with my labors. He left and retreated,
He lived his life a little while longer:
65 Yet his right-hand guarded his footstep in Heorot,
And sad-mooded thence to the sea-bottom fell he,
Mournful in mind. For the might-rush of battle
The friend of the Scyldings, with gold that was plated,
With ornaments many, much requited me,
70 When daylight had dawned, and down to the banquet
We had sat us together. There was chanting and joyance:
The age-stricken Scylding asked many questions

Having made these preliminary statements, I will now tell thee of Grendel, the monster.

Hondscio fell first.

I reflected honor upon my people.

King Hrothgar lavished gifts upon me.

And of old-times related ; oft light-ringing harp-strings,
Joy-telling wood, were touched by the brave one ;
75 Now he uttered measures, mourning and truthful,
Then the large-hearted land-king a legend of wonder
Truthfully told us.   Now troubled with years

The age-hoary warrior afterward began to
Mourn for the might that marked him in youth-days ;
80 His breast within boiled, when burdened with winters
Much he remembered.   From morning till night then
We joyed us therein as etiquette suffered,
Till the second night season came unto earth-folk.
Then early thereafter, the mother of Grendel

85 Was ready for vengeance, wretched she journeyed ;
Her son had death ravished, the wrath of the Geatmen.
The horrible woman avengèd her offspring,
And with mighty mainstrength murdered a hero.

There the spirit of Æschere, agèd adviser,
90 Was ready to vanish ; nor when morn had lightened
Were they anywise suffered to consume him with fire,
Folk of the Danemen, the death-weakened hero,
Nor the belovèd liegeman to lay on the pyre ;

She the corpse had offcarried in the clutch of the foeman[1]
95 'Neath mountain-brook's flood.   To Hrothgar 'twas saddest
Of pains that ever had preyed on the chieftain ;
By the life of thee the land-prince then me[2]
Besought very sadly, in sea-currents' eddies
To display my prowess, to peril my safety,
100 Might-deeds accomplish ; much did he promise.

I found then the famous flood-current's cruel,
Horrible depth-warder.   A while unto us two

---

[1] For ' fæðmum,' Gr.'s conjecture, B. proposes ' færunga.'   These three
half-verses would then read: *She bore off the corpse of her foe suddenly under
the mountain-torrent.*

[2] The phrase ' þíne lýfe ' (2132) was long rendered ' *with thy (presupposed)
permission.*'   The verse would read: *The land-prince then sadly besought me,
with thy (presupposed) permission, etc.*

Hand was in common; the currents were seething
With gore that was clotted, and Grendel's fierce mother's
105 Head I offhacked in the hall at the bottom
With huge-reaching sword-edge, hardly I wrested
My life from her clutches; not doomed was I then,
But the warden of earlmen afterward gave me
Jewels in quantity, kinsman of Healfdene.

and hewed her head off.

Jewels were freely bestowed upon me.

XXXI.

GIFT-GIVING IS MUTUAL.

" So the belovèd land-prince lived in decorum;
I had missed no rewards, no meeds of my prowess,
But he gave me jewels, regarding my wishes,
Healfdene his bairn; I'll bring them to thee, then,
5 Atheling of earlmen, offer them gladly.
And still unto thee is all my affection:[1]
But few of my folk-kin find I surviving
But thee, dear Higelac!" Bade he in then to carry[2]
The boar-image, banner, battle-high helmet,
10 Iron-gray armor, the excellent weapon,
In song-measures said: " This suit-for-the-battle
Hrothgar presented me, bade me expressly,
Wise-mooded atheling, thereafter to tell thee[3]
The whole of its history, said King Heregar owned it,
15 Dane-prince for long: yet he wished not to give then

All my gifts I lay at thy feet.

This armor I have belonged of yore to Heregar.

---

[1] This verse B. renders, '*Now serve I again thee alone as my gracious king.*'

[2] For 'eafor' (2153), Kl. suggests 'ealdor.' Translate then: *Bade the prince then to bear in the banner, battle-high helmet, etc.* On the other hand, W. takes 'eaforhéafodsegn' as a compound, meaning 'helmet': *He bade them bear in the helmet, battle-high helm, gray armor, etc.*

[3] The H.-So. rendering (*ærest = history, origin; 'eft' for 'est'*), though liable to objection, is perhaps the best offered. 'That I should very early tell thee of his favor, kindness' sounds well; but 'his' is badly placed to limit 'ést.'— Perhaps, 'eft' with verbs of saying may have the force of Lat. prefix 're,' and the H.-So. reading mean, 'that I should its origin rehearse to thee.'

The mail to his son, though dearly he loved him,
Hereward the hardy.   Hold all in joyance !"
I heard that there followed hard on the jewels
Two braces of stallions of striking resemblance,
20 Dappled and yellow ; he granted him usance
Of horses and treasures.   So a kinsman should bear him,
No web of treachery weave for another,
Nor by cunning craftiness cause the destruction

Of trusty companion.   Most precious to Higelac,
25 The bold one in battle, was the bairn of his sister,
And each unto other mindful of favors.

I am told that to Hygd he proffered the necklace,
Wonder-gem rare that Wealhtheow gave him,
The troop-leader's daughter, a trio of horses
30 Slender and saddle-bright ; soon did the jewel
Embellish her bosom, when the beer-feast was over.
So Ecgtheow's bairn brave did prove him,

War-famous man, by deeds that were valiant,
He lived in honor, belovèd companions
35 Slew not carousing ; his mood was not cruel,
But by hand-strength hugest of heroes then living
The brave one retained the bountiful gift that
The Lord had allowed him.   Long was he wretched,
So that sons of the Geatmen accounted him worthless,
40 And the lord of the liegemen loth was to do him
Mickle of honor, when mead-cups were passing ;
They fully believed him idle and sluggish,

An indolent atheling : to the honor-blest man there
Came requital for the cuts he had suffered.
45 The folk-troop's defender bade fetch to the building
The heirloom of Hrethel, embellished with gold,

So the brave one enjoined it ; there was jewel no richer
In the form of a weapon 'mong Geats of that era ;
In Beowulf's keeping he placed it and gave him
50 Seven of thousands, manor and lordship.
Common to both was land 'mong the people,

Estate and inherited rights and possessions,
To the second one specially spacious dominions,
To the one who was better.   It afterward happened
55 In days that followed, befell the battle-thanes,
After Higelac's death, and when Heardred was murdered

After Heardred's
death, Beowulf be-
comes king.

With weapons of warfare 'neath well-covered targets,
When valiant battlemen in victor-band sought him,
War-Scylfing heroes harassed the nephew
60 Of Hereric in battle.   To Beowulf's keeping
Turned there in time extensive dominions :
He fittingly ruled them a fifty of winters

He rules the Geats
fifty years.

(He a man-ruler wise was, manor-ward old) till
A certain one 'gan, on gloom-darkening nights, a
65 Dragon, to govern, who guarded a treasure,

The fire-drake.

A high-rising stone-cliff, on heath that was grayish :
A path 'neath it lay, unknown unto mortals.
Some one of earthmen entered the mountain,
The heathenish hoard laid hold of with ardor ;

*   *   *   *   *   *   *
*   *   *   *   *   *   *
*   *   *   *   *   *   *
*   *   *   *   *   *   *
*   *   *   *   *   *   *

XXXII.

THE HOARD AND THE DRAGON.

*   *   *   *   *   *   *

He sought of himself who sorely did harm him,
But, for need very pressing, the servant of one of
The sons of the heroes hate-blows evaded,
5 Seeking for shelter and the sin-driven warrior
Took refuge within there.   He early looked in it,

*   *   *   *   *   *   *
*   *   *   *   *   *   *

    *   *   *   *   *   when the onset surprised him,

10 He a gem-vessel saw there : many of suchlike
Ancient ornaments in the earth-cave were lying,
As in days of yore some one of men of
Illustrious lineage, as a legacy monstrous,
There had secreted them, careful and thoughtful,

15 Dear-valued jewels. Death had offsnatched them,
In the days of the past, and the one man moreover
Of the flower of the folk who fared there the longest,
Was fain to defer it, friend-mourning warder,
A little longer to be left in enjoyment

20 Of long-lasting treasure.[1] A barrow all-ready
Stood on the plain the stream-currents nigh to,
New by the ness-edge, unnethe of approaching :
The keeper of rings carried within a
[2] Ponderous deal of the treasure of nobles,

25 Of gold that was beaten, briefly he spake then :[3]

The ring-giver be-
wails the loss of
retainers.

  " Hold thou, O Earth, now heroes no more may,
The earnings of earlmen. Lo ! erst in thy bosom
Worthy men won them ; war-death hath ravished,
Perilous life-bale, all my warriors,

30 Liegemen belovèd, who this life have forsaken,
Who hall-pleasures saw. No sword-bearer have I,
And no one to burnish the gold-plated vessel,
The high-valued beaker : my heroes are vanished.
The hardy helmet behung with gilding

35 Shall be reaved of its riches : the ring-cleansers slumber
Who were charged to have ready visors-for-battle,
And the burnie that bided in battle-encounter

---

[1] For 'long-gestréona,' B. suggests 'láengestréona,' and renders, *Of fleeting treasures.* S. accepts H.'s 'long-gestréona, but renders, *The treasure long in accumulating.*

[2] For 'hard-fyrdne' (2246), B. first suggested 'hard-fyndne,' rendering : *A heap of treasures . . . so great that its equal would be hard to find.* The same scholar suggests later 'hord-wynne dæl' = *A deal of treasure-joy.*

[3] Some read 'fec-word' (2247), and render : *Banning words uttered.*

O'er breaking of war-shields the bite of the edges
Moulds with the hero. The ring-twisted armor,
40 Its lord being lifeless, no longer may journey
Hanging by heroes; harp-joy is vanished,
The rapture of glee-wood, no excellent falcon
Swoops through the building, no swift-footed charger
Grindeth the gravel. A grievous destruction
45 No few of the world-folk widely hath scattered !"
So, woful of spirit one after all
Lamented mournfully, moaning in sadness
By day and by night, till death with its billows
Dashed on his spirit. Then the ancient dusk-scather   The fire-dragon.
50 Found the great treasure standing all open,
He who flaming and fiery flies to the barrows,
Naked war-dragon, nightly escapeth
Encompassed with fire; men under heaven
Widely beheld him. 'Tis said that he looks for [1]
55 The hoard in the earth, where old he is guarding
The heathenish treasure; he'll be nowise the better.
So three-hundred winters the waster of peoples   The dragon meets
Held upon earth that excellent hoard-hall,   his match.
Till the forementioned earlman angered him bitterly :
60 The beat-plated beaker he bare to his chieftain
And fullest remission for all his remissness
Begged of his liegelord. Then the hoard [2] was discovered,
The treasure was taken, his petition was granted
The lorn-mooded liegeman. His lord regarded   The hero plunders
65 The old-work of earth-folk — 'twas the earliest occasion.   the dragon's den.
When the dragon awoke, the strife was renewed there ;
He snuffed 'long the stone then, stout-hearted found he

---

[1] An earlier reading of H.'s gave the following meaning to this passage:
He is said to inhabit a mound under the earth, where he, etc. The translation
in the text is more authentic.

[2] The repetition of 'hord' in this passage has led some scholars to suggest
new readings to avoid the second 'hord.' This, however, is not under the
main stress, and, it seems to me, might easily be accepted.

The footprint of foeman ; too far had he gone
With cunning craftiness close to the head of
70 The fire-spewing dragon.   So undoomed he may 'scape from
Anguish and exile with ease who possesseth
The favor of Heaven.   The hoard-warden eagerly
Searched o'er the ground then, would meet with the person
That caused him sorrow while in slumber reclining :
75 Gleaming and wild he oft went round the cavern,
All of it outward ; not any of earthmen
Was seen in that desert.[1]   Yet he joyed in the battle,
Rejoiced in the conflict : oft he turned to the barrow,
Sought for the gem-cup ;[2] this he soon perceived then

The dragon per-
ceives that some
one has disturbed
his treasure.

80 That some man or other had discovered the gold,
The famous folk-treasure.   Not fain did the hoard-ward
Wait until evening ; then the ward of the barrow
Was angry in spirit, the loathèd one wished to
Pay for the dear-valued drink-cup with fire.
85 Then the day was done as the dragon would have it,
He no longer would wait on the wall, but departed

The dragon is in-
furiated.

Fire-impelled, flaming.   Fearful the start was
To earls in the land, as it early thereafter
To their giver-of-gold was grievously ended.

XXXIII.

BRAVE THOUGH AGED. — REMINISCENCES.

The dragon spits
fire.

The stranger began then to vomit forth fire,
To burn the great manor ; the blaze then glimmered
For anguish to earlmen, not anything living

---

[1] The reading of H.-So. is well defended in the notes to that volume.   B.
emends and renders: *Nor was there any man in that desert who rejoiced in
conflict, in battle-work.*   That is, the hoard-ward could not find any one who
had disturbed his slumbers, for no warrior was there.   t. B.'s emendation
would give substantially the same translation.

[2] 'Sinc-fæt' (2301) : this word both here and in v. 2232, t. B. renders
'treasure.'

Was the hateful air-goer willing to leave there.
5   The war of the worm widely was noticed,
The feud of the foeman afar and anear,
How the enemy injured the earls of the Geatmen,
Harried with hatred : back he hied to the treasure,
To the well-hidden cavern ere the coming of daylight.
10 He had circled with fire the folk of those regions,
With brand and burning ; in the barrow he trusted,
In the wall and his war-might : the weening deceived him.
Then straight was the horror to Beowulf published,   *Beowulf hears of the havoc wrought by the dragon.*
Early forsooth, that his own native homestead,[1]
15 The best of buildings, was burning and melting,
Gift-seat of Geatmen. 'Twas a grief to the spirit
Of the good-mooded hero, the greatest of sorrows :
The wise one weened then that wielding his kingdom   *He fears that Heaven is punishing him for some crime.*
'Gainst the ancient commandments, he had bitterly angered
20 The Lord everlasting : with lorn meditations
His bosom welled inward, as was nowise his custom.
The fire-spewing dragon fully had wasted
The fastness of warriors, the water-land outward,
The manor with fire. The folk-ruling hero,
25 Prince of the Weders, was planning to wreak him.
The warmen's defender bade them to make him,
Earlmen's atheling, an excellent war-shield
Wholly of iron : fully he knew then   *He orders an iron shield to be made for him; wood is useless.*
That wood from the forest was helpless to aid him,
30 Shield against fire. The long-worthy ruler
Must live the last of his limited earth-days,
Of life in the world and the worm along with him,
Though he long had been holding hoard-wealth in plenty.
Then the ring-prince disdained to seek with a war-band,   *He determines to fight alone.*
35 With army extensive, the air-going ranger ;
He felt no fear of the foeman's assaults and
He counted for little the might of the dragon,

---

[1] 'Hám' (2326), the suggestion of B. is accepted by t. B. and other scholars.

His power and prowess : for previously dared he

Beowulf's early
triumphs referred
to.

A heap of hostility, hazarded dangers,

40 War-thane, when Hrothgar's palace he cleansèd,

Conquering combatant, clutched in the battle

The kinsmen of Grendel, of kindred detested.[1]

Higelac's death
recalled.

'Twas of hand-fights not least where Higelac was slaughtered,

When the king of the Geatmen with clashings of battle,

45 Friend-lord of folks in Frisian dominions,

Offspring of Hrethrel perished through sword-drink,

With battle-swords beaten ; thence Beowulf came then

On self-help relying, swam through the waters ;

He bare on his arm, lone-going, thirty

50 Outfits of armor, when the ocean he mounted.

The Hetwars by no means had need to be boastful

Of their fighting afoot, who forward to meet him

Carried their war-shields : not many returned from

The brave-mooded battle-knight back to their homesteads.

55 Ecgtheow's bairn o'er the bight-courses swam then,

Lone-goer lorn to his land-folk returning,

Where Hygd to him tendered treasure and kingdom,

Heardred's lack of
capacity to rule.

Rings and dominion : her son she not trusted,

To be able to keep the kingdom devised him

60 'Gainst alien races, on the death of King Higelac.

Beowulf's tact and
delicacy recalled.

Yet the sad ones succeeded not in persuading the atheling

In any way ever, to act as a suzerain

To Heardred, or promise to govern the kingdom ;

Yet with friendly counsel in the folk he sustained him,

65 Gracious, with honor, till he grew to be older,

Reference is here
made to a visit
which Beowulf re-
ceives from Ean-
mund and Eadgils;
why they come is
not known.

Wielded the Weders. Wide-fleeing outlaws,

Ohthere's sons, sought him o'er the waters :

They had stirred a revolt 'gainst the helm of the Scylfings,

The best of the sea-kings, who in Swedish dominions

70 Distributed treasure, distinguished folk-leader.

---

[1] For 'láðan cynnes' (2355), t. B. suggests 'láðan cynne,' apposition to
' mægum.' From syntactical and other considerations, this is a most excellent
emendation.

'Twas the end of his earth-days ; injury fatal [1]
By swing of the sword he received as a greeting,
Offspring of Higelac ; Ongentheow's bairn
Later departed to visit his homestead,
75 When Heardred was dead ; let Beowulf rule them,
Govern the Geatmen : good was that folk-king.

XXXIV.

BEOWULF SEEKS THE DRAGON.—BEOWULF'S REMINISCENCES.

He planned requital for the folk-leader's ruin
In days thereafter, to Eadgils the wretched
Becoming an enemy.   Ohthere's son then
Went with a war-troop o'er the wide-stretching currents
5 With warriors and weapons : with woe-journeys cold he
After avenged him, the king's life he took.
So he came off uninjured from all of his battles,

Perilous fights, offspring of Ecgtheow,

Beowulf has been preserved through many perils.

From his deeds of daring, till that day most momentous
10 When he fate-driven fared to fight with the dragon.
With eleven companions the prince of the Geatmen
Went lowering with fury to look at the fire-drake :

With eleven comrades, he seeks the dragon.

Inquiring he'd found how the feud had arisen,
Hate to his heroes ; the highly-famed gem-vessel
15 Was brought to his keeping through the hand of th' informer.
That in the throng was thirteenth of heroes,

A guide leads the way, but

That caused the beginning of conflict so bitter,
Captive and wretched, must sad-mooded thenceward
Point out the place : he passed then unwillingly

very reluctantly.

20 To the spot where he knew of the notable cavern,
The cave under earth, not far from the ocean,
The anger of eddies, which inward was full of
Jewels and wires : a warden uncanny,

---

[1] Gr. read 'on feorme ' (2386), rendering: *He there at the banquet a fatal wound received by blows of the sword.*

Warrior weaponed, wardered the treasure,
25   Old under earth ; no easy possession
For any of earth-folk access to get to.
Then the battle-brave atheling sat on the naze-edge,
While the gold-friend of Geatmen gracious saluted
His fireside-companions : woe was his spirit,
30   Death-boding, wav'ring ; Weird very near him,
Who must seize the old hero, his soul-treasure look for,
Dragging aloof his life from his body :
Not flesh-hidden long was the folk-leader's spirit.
Beowulf spake, Ecgtheow's son :

Beowulf's retro-
spect.
35   " I survived in my youth-days many a conflict,
Hours of onset: that all I remember.
I was seven-winters old when the jewel-prince took me,
High-lord of heroes, at the hands of my father,
Hrethel the hero-king had me in keeping,

Hrethel took me
when I was seven.
40   Gave me treasure and feasting, our kinship remembered ;
Not ever was I *any* less dear to him

He treated me as
a son.
Knight in the boroughs, than the bairns of his household,
Herebald and Hæthcyn and Higelac mine.
To the eldest unjustly by acts of a kinsman
45   Was murder-bed strewn, since him Hæthcyn from horn-bow

One of the brothers
accidentally kills
another.
His sheltering chieftain shot with an arrow,
Erred in his aim and injured his kinsman,
One brother the other, with blood-sprinkled spear :

No fee could com-
pound for such a
calamity.
'Twas a feeless fight, finished in malice,
50   Sad to his spirit ; the folk-prince however
Had to part from existence with vengeance untaken.

[A parallel case
is supposed.]
So to hoar-headed hero 'tis heavily crushing [1]

---

[1] 'Gomelum ceorle' (2445).— II. takes these words as referring to Hrethel;
but the translator here departs from his editor by understanding the poet to
refer to a hypothetical old man, introduced as an illustration of a father's
sorrow.

Hrethrel had certainly never seen a son of his ride on the gallows to feed
the crows.

The passage beginning 'swá biⸯ géomorlic' seems to be an effort to reach

To live to see his son as he rideth
Young on the gallows : then measures he chanteth,
55 A song of sorrow, when his son is hanging
For the raven's delight, and aged and hoary
He is unable to offer any assistance.
Every morning his offspring's departure
Is constant recalled : he cares not to wait for
60 The birth of an heir in his borough-enclosures,
Since that one through death-pain the deeds hath experienced.
He heart-grieved beholds in the house of his son the
Wine-building wasted, the wind-lodging places
Reaved of their roaring ; the riders are sleeping,
65 The knights in the grave ; there's no sound of the harp-wood,
Joy in the yards, as of yore were familiar.

XXXV.

REMINISCENCES *(continued)*. — BEOWULF'S LAST BATTLE.

" He seeks then his chamber, singeth a woe-song
One for the other ; all too extensive
Seemed homesteads and plains.   So the helm of the Weders
Mindful of Herebald heart-sorrow carried,

Hrethel grieves
for Herebald.

5 Stirred with emotion, nowise was able
To wreak his ruin on the ruthless destroyer :
He was unable to follow the warrior with hatred,
With deeds that were direful, though dear he not held him.

a full simile, 'as . . . so.'   'As it is mournful for an old man, etc. . . . so the
defence of the Weders (2463) bore heart-sorrow, etc.'   The verses 2451 to
2463½ would be parenthetical, the poet's feelings being so strong as to inter-
rupt the simile.   The punctuation of the fourth edition would be better — a
comma after 'galgan' (2447).   The translation may be indicated as follows :
*(Just) as it is sad for an old man to see his son ride young on the gallows when
he himself is uttering mournful measures, a sorrowful song, while his son hangs
for a comfort to the raven, and he, old and infirm, cannot render him any
help* — (he is constantly reminded, etc., 2451-2463) — *so the defence of the
Weders, etc.*

Then pressed by the pang this pain occasioned him,
10　He gave up glee, God-light elected;
He left to his sons, as the man that is rich does,
His land and fortress, when from life he departed.

Strife between
Swedes and Geats.
Then was crime and hostility 'twixt Swedes and Geatmen,
O'er wide-stretching water warring was mutual,
15　Burdensome hatred, when Hrethel had perished,
And Ongentheow's offspring were active and valiant,
Wished not to hold to peace oversea, but
Round Hreosna-beorh often accomplished
Cruelest massacre.　This my kinsman avengèd,
20　The feud and fury, as 'tis found on inquiry,
Though one of them paid it with forfeit of life-joys,

Hæthcyn's fall at
Ravenswood.
With price that was hard: the struggle became then
Fatal to Hæthcyn, lord of the Geatmen.
Then I heard that at morning one brother the other
25　With edges of irons egged on to murder,
Where Ongentheow maketh onset on Eofor:
The helmet crashed, the hoary-haired Scylfing
Sword-smitten fell, his hand then remembered
Feud-hate sufficient, refused not the death-blow.

I requited him for
the jewels he gave
me.
30　The gems that he gave me, with jewel-bright sword I
'Quited in contest, as occasion was offered:
Land he allowed me, life-joy at homestead,
Manor to live on.　Little he needed
From Gepids or Danes or in Sweden to look for
35　Trooper less true, with treasure to buy him;
'Mong foot-soldiers ever in front I would hie me,
Alone in the vanguard, and evermore gladly
Warfare shall wage, while this weapon endureth
That late and early often did serve me

Beowulf refers to
his having slain
Dæghrefn.
40　When I proved before heroes the slayer of Dæghrefn,
Knight of the Hugmen: he by no means was suffered
To the king of the Frisians to carry the jewels,
The breast-decoration; but the banner-possessor
Bowed in the battle, brave-mooded atheling.

45 No weapon was slayer, but war-grapple broke then
The surge of his spirit, his body destroying.
Now shall weapon's edge make war for the treasure,
And hand and firm-sword." Beowulf spake then,
Boast-words uttered — the latest occasion :

50 " I braved in my youth-days battles unnumbered ;
Still am I willing the struggle to look for,
Fame-deeds perform, folk-warden prudent,
If the hateful despoiler forth from his cavern
Seeketh me out ! " Each of the heroes,

55 Helm-bearers sturdy, he thereupon greeted
Belovèd co-liegemen — his last salutation :
" No brand would I bear, no blade for the dragon,
Wist I a way my word-boast to 'complish [1]
Else with the monster, as with Grendel I did it ;

60 But fire in the battle hot I expect there,
Furious flame-burning : so I fixed on my body
Target and war-mail. The ward of the barrow [2]
I'll not flee from a foot-length, the foeman uncanny.
At the wall 'twill befall us as Fate decreeth,

65 Each one's Creator. I am eager in spirit,
With the wingèd war-hero to away with all boasting.
Bide on the barrow with burnies protected,
Earls in armor, which of *us* two may better
Bear his disaster, when the battle is over.

70 'Tis no matter of yours, and man cannot do it,
But me and me only, to measure his strength with
The monster of malice, might-deeds to 'complish.
I with prowess shall gain the gold, or the battle,

*He boasts of his
youthful prowess,
and declares him-
self still fearless.*

*His last saluta-
tions.*

*Let Fate decide
between us.*

*Wait ye here till
the battle is over.*

---

[1] The clause 2520(2)–2522(1), rendered by 'Wist I . . . monster,' Gr.,
followed by S., translates substantially as follows : *If I knew how else I might
combat the boastful defiance of the monster.* — The translation turns upon
' wiðgrípan,' a word not understood.

[2] B. emends and translates : *I will not flee the space of a foot from the guard
of the barrow, but there shall be to us a fight at the wall, as Fate decrees, each
one's Creator.*

Direful death-woe will drag off your ruler !"

75 The mighty champion rose by his shield then,
Brave under helmet, in battle-mail went he
'Neath steep-rising stone-cliffs, the strength he relied on
Of one man alone : no work for a coward.
Then he saw by the wall who a great many battles

80 Had lived through, most worthy, when foot-troops collided,

The place of strife is described.

Stone-arches standing, stout-hearted champion,
Saw a brook from the barrow bubbling out thenceward :
The flood of the fountain was fuming with war-flame :
Not nigh to the hoard, for season the briefest

85 Could he brave, without burning, the abyss that was yawning,
The drake was so fiery. The prince of the Weders
Caused then that words came from his bosom,
So fierce was his fury ; the firm-hearted shouted :
His battle-clear voice came in resounding

90 'Neath the gray-colored stone. Stirred was his hatred,

Beowulf calls out under the stone arches.

The hoard-ward distinguished the speech of a man ;
Time was no longer to look out for friendship.
The breath of the monster issued forth first,
Vapory war-sweat, out of the stone-cave :

The terrible encounter.

95 The earth re-echoed. The earl 'neath the barrow
Lifted his shield, lord of the Geatmen,
Tow'rd the terrible stranger : the ring-twisted creature's
Heart was then ready to seek for a struggle.

Beowulf brandishes his sword,

The excellent battle-king first brandished his weapon,

100 The ancient heirloom, of edges unblunted,[1]
To the death-planners twain was terror from other.

and stands against his shield.

The lord of the troopers intrepidly stood then
'Gainst his high-rising shield, when the dragon coiled him

The dragon coils himself.

Quickly together : in corslet he bided.

---

[1] The translation of this passage is based on 'unsláw' (2565), accepted by H.-So., in lieu of the long-standing 'ungléaw.' The former is taken as an adj. limiting 'sweord'; the latter as an adj. c. 'góð-cyning': *The good war-king, rash with edges, brandished his sword, his old relic.* The latter gives a more rhetorical Anglo-Saxon (poetical) sentence.

105 He went then in blazes, bended and striding,
   Hasting him forward. His life and body
   The targe well protected, for time-period shorter
   Than wish demanded for the well-renowned leader,
   Where he then for the first day was forced to be victor,
110 Famous in battle, as Fate had not willed it.
   The lord of the Geatmen uplifted his hand then,
   Smiting the fire-drake with sword that was precious,
   That bright on the bone the blade-edge did weaken,
   Bit more feebly than his folk-leader needed,
115 Burdened with bale-griefs. Then the barrow-protector,   *The dragon rages.*
   When the sword-blow had fallen, was fierce in his spirit,
   Flinging his fires, flamings of battle
   Gleamed then afar : the gold-friend of Weders
   Boasted no conquests, his battle-sword failed him   *Beowulf's sword*
120 Naked in conflict, as by no means it ought to,   *fails him.*
   Long-trusty weapon. 'Twas no slight undertaking
   That Ecgtheow's famous offspring would leave
   The drake-cavern's bottom ; he must live in some region
   Other than this, by the will of the dragon,
125 As each one of earthmen existence must forfeit.
   'Twas early thereafter the excellent warriors
   Met with each other. Anew and afresh   *The combat is*
   The hoard-ward took heart (gasps heaved then his bosom) :   *renewed.*
   Sorrow he suffered encircled with fire   *The great hero is*
                                                                  reduced to extrem-
130 Who the people erst governed. His companions by no means   *ities.*
   Were banded about him, bairns of the princes,
   With valorous spirit, but they sped to the forest,   *His comrades flee!*
   Seeking for safety. The soul-deeps of one were
   Ruffled by care : kin-love can never   *Blood is thicker*
                                                                  than water.
135 Aught in him waver who well doth consider.

XXXVI.

WIGLAF THE TRUSTY. — BEOWULF IS DESERTED BY FRIENDS AND BY SWORD.

Wiglaf remains
true — the ideal
Teutonic liege-
man.

The son of Weohstan was Wiglaf entitled,
Shield-warrior precious, prince of the Scylfings,
Ælfhere's kinsman : he saw his dear liegelord
Enduring the heat 'neath helmet and visor.

Wiglaf recalls
Beowulf's gener-
osity.

5 Then he minded the holding that erst he had given him,
The Wægmunding warriors' wealth-blessèd homestead,
Each of the folk-rights his father had wielded ;
He was hot for the battle, his hand seized the target,
The yellow-bark shield, he unsheathed his old weapon,
10 Which was known among earthmen as the relic of Eanmund,
Ohthere's offspring, whom, exiled and friendless,
Weohstan did slay with sword-edge in battle,
And carried his kinsman the clear-shining helmet,
The ring-made burnie, the old giant-weapon
15 That Onela gave him, his boon-fellow's armor,
Ready war-trappings : he the feud did not mention,
Though he'd fatally smitten the son of his brother.
Many a half-year held he the treasures,
The bill and the burnie, till his bairn became able,
20 Like his father before him, fame-deeds to 'complish ;
Then he gave him 'mong Geatmen a goodly array of
Weeds for his warfare ; he went from life then
Old on his journey.   'Twas the earliest time then

This is Wiglaf's
first battle as liege-
man of Beowulf.

That the youthful champion might charge in the battle
25 Aiding his liegelord ; his spirit was dauntless.
Nor did kinsman's bequest quail at the battle :
This the dragon discovered on their coming together.
Wiglaf uttered many a right-saying,
Said to his fellows, sad was his spirit :

Wiglaf appeals to
the pride of the
cowards.

30 " I remember the time when, tasting the mead-cup,
We promised in the hall the lord of us all

Who gave us these ring-treasures, that this battle-equipment,
Swords and helmets, we'd certainly quite him,
Should need of such aid ever befall him :

35 In the war-band he chose us for this journey spontaneously,
Stirred us to glory and gave me these jewels,
Since he held and esteemed us trust-worthy spearmen,
Hardy helm-bearers, though this hero-achievement
Our lord intended alone to accomplish,

40 Ward of his people, for most of achievements,
Doings audacious, he did among earth-folk.
The day is now come when the ruler of earthmen
Needeth the vigor of valiant heroes :
Let us wend us towards him, the war-prince to succor,

45 While the heat yet rageth, horrible fire-fight.
God wot in me, 'tis mickle the liefer
The blaze should embrace my body and eat it
With my treasure-bestower. Meseemeth not proper
To bear our battle-shields back to our country,

50 'Less first we are able to fell and destroy the
Long-hating foeman, to defend the life of
The prince of the Weders. Well do I know 'tisn't
Earned by his exploits, he only of Geatmen
Sorrow should suffer, sink in the battle :

55 Brand and helmet to us both shall be common,
¹ Shield-cover, burnie." Through the bale-smoke he stalked
     then,
Went under helmet to the help of his chieftain,
Briefly discoursing : " Beowulf dear,
Perform thou all fully, as thou formerly saidst,

60 In thy youthful years, that while yet thou livedst

Marginal notes:

How we have forfeited our liege-lord's confidence!

Our lord is in sore need of us.

I would rather die than go home without my suzerain.

Surely he does not deserve to die alone.

Wiglaf reminds Beowulf of his youthful boasts.

---

¹ The passage ‘*Brand ... burnie,*’ is much disputed. In the first place, some eminent critics assume a gap of at least two half-verses. — ‘Úrum’ (2660), being a peculiar form, has been much discussed. ‘Byrdu-scrûd’ is also a crux. B. suggests ‘bȳwdu-scrûd’ = *splendid vestments.* Nor is ‘bám’ accepted by all, ‘béon’ being suggested. Whatever the individual words, the passage must mean, “ *I intend to share with him my equipments of defence.*”

Beowulf.

Thou wouldst let thine honor not ever be lessened.
Thy life thou shalt save, mighty in actions,
Atheling undaunted, with all of thy vigor ;

The monster advances on them.
I'll give thee assistance." The dragon came raging,

65 Wild-mooded stranger, when these words had been uttered
('Twas the second occasion), seeking his enemies,
Men that were hated, with hot-gleaming fire-waves ;
With blaze-billows burned the board to its edges :
The fight-armor failed then to furnish assistance

70 To the youthful spear-hero : but the young-agèd stripling
Quickly advanced 'neath his kinsman's war-target,
Since his own had been ground in the grip of the fire.

Beowulf strikes at the dragon.
Then the warrior-king was careful of glory,
He soundly smote with sword-for-the-battle,

75 That it stood in the head by hatred ydriven ;
Nægling was shivered, the old and iron-made

His sword fails him.
Brand of Beowulf in battle deceived him.
'Twas denied him that edges of irons were able
To help in the battle ; the hand was too mighty

80 [1] Which every weapon, as I heard on inquiry,
Outstruck in its stroke, when to struggle he carried
The wonderful war-sword : it waxed him no better.

The dragon advances on Beowulf again.
Then the people-despoiler — third of his onsets —
Fierce-raging fire-drake, of feud-hate was mindful,

85 Charged on the strong one, when chance was afforded,
Heated and war-grim, seized on his neck
With teeth that were bitter ; he bloody did wax with
Soul-gore seething ; sword-blood in waves boiled.

---

[1] B. would render: *Which, as I heard, excelled in stroke every sword that he carried to the strife, even the strongest (sword).* For 'þonne' he reads 'þone,' rel. pr.

XXXVII.

THE FATAL STRUGGLE. — BEOWULF'S LAST MOMENTS.

Then I heard that at need of the king of the people   Wiglaf defends
The upstanding earlman exhibited prowess,   Beowulf.
Vigor and courage, as suited his nature ;
[1] He his head did not guard, but the high-minded liegeman's
5 Hand was consumed, when he succored his kinsman,
So he struck the strife-bringing strange-comer lower,
Earl-thane in armor, that *in* went the weapon
Gleaming and plated, that 'gan then the fire [2]
Later to lessen. The liegelord himself then   Beowulf draws
10 Retained his consciousness, brandished his war-knife,   his knife,
Battle-sharp, bitter, that he bare on his armor :
The Weder-lord cut the worm in the middle.   and cuts the
They had felled the enemy (life drove out then [3]   dragon.
Puissant prowess), the pair had destroyed him,
15 Land-chiefs related : so a liegeman should prove him,
A thaneman when needed. To the prince 'twas the last of
His era of conquest by his own great achievements,

---

[1] B. renders: *He* (*W.*) *did not regard his* (*the dragon's*) *head* (since
Beowulf had struck it without effect), *but struck the dragon a little lower down.*
— One crux is to find out *whose head* is meant; another is to bring out the
antithesis between 'head' and 'hand.'

[2] 'þæt þæt fýr' (2702), S. emends to 'þá þæt fýr' = *when the fire began to
grow less intense afterward.* This emendation relieves the passage of a
plethora of conjunctive þæt's.

[3] For 'gefyldan' (2707), S. proposes 'gefylde.' The passage would read :
*He felled the foe (life drove out strength), and they then both had destroyed him,
chieftains related.* This gives Beowulf the credit of having felled the dragon ;
then they combine to annihilate him. — For 'ellen' (2707), Kl. suggests
'e(a)llne.' — The reading '*life drove out strength*' is very unsatisfactory and
very peculiar. I would suggest as follows : Adopt S.'s emendation, remove
H.'s parenthesis, read 'ferh-ellen wræc,' and translate : *He felled the foe,
drove out his life-strength* (that is, made him *hors de combat*), *and then they
both, etc.*

Beowulf's wound swells and burns.

The latest of world-deeds. The wound then began
Which the earth-dwelling dragon erstwhile had wrought him
20 To burn and to swell. He soon then discovered
That bitterest bale-woe in his bosom was raging,
Poison within. The atheling advanced then,

He sits down exhausted.

That along by the wall, he prudent of spirit
Might sit on a settle; he saw the giant-work,
25 How arches of stone strengthened with pillars
The earth-hall eternal inward supported.
Then the long-worthy liegeman laved with his hand the

Wiglaf bathes his lord's head.

Far-famous chieftain, gory from sword-edge,
Refreshing the face of his friend-lord and ruler,
30 Sated with battle, unbinding his helmet.
Beowulf answered, of his injury spake he,
His wound that was fatal (he was fully aware
He had lived his allotted life-days enjoying
The pleasures of earth; then past was entirely
35 His measure of days, death very near):

Beowulf regrets that he has no son.

"My son I would give now my battle-equipments,
Had any of heirs been after me granted,
Along of my body. This people I governed
Fifty of winters: no king 'mong my neighbors
40 Dared to encounter me with comrades-in-battle,
Try me with terror. The time to me ordered
I bided at home, mine own kept fitly,
Sought me no snares, swore me not many

I can rejoice in a well-spent life.

Oaths in injustice. Joy over all this
45 I'm able to have, though ill with my death-wounds;
Hence the Ruler of Earthmen need not charge me
With the killing of kinsmen, when cometh my life out
Forth from my body. Fare thou with haste now

Bring me the hoard, Wiglaf, that my dying eyes may be refreshed by a sight of it.

To behold the hoard 'neath the hoar-grayish stone,
50 Well-lovèd Wiglaf, now the worm is a-lying,
Sore-wounded sleepeth, disseized of his treasure.
Go thou in haste that treasures of old I,
Gold-wealth may gaze on, together see lying

The ether-bright jewels, be easier able,
55 Having the heap of hoard-gems, to yield my
Life and the land-folk whom long I have governed."

XXXVIII.

WIGLAF PLUNDERS THE DRAGON'S DEN. — BEOWULF'S DEATH.

Then heard I that Wihstan's son very quickly,
These words being uttered, heeded his liegelord
Wounded and war-sick, went in his armor,
His well-woven ring-mail, 'neath the roof of the barrow.
5 Then the trusty retainer treasure-gems many
Victorious saw, when the seat he came near to.
Gold-treasure sparkling spread on the bottom,
Wonder on the wall, and the worm-creature's cavern,
The ancient dawn-flier's, vessels a-standing,
10 Cups of the ancients of cleansers bereavèd,
Robbed of their ornaments: there were helmets in numbers,
Old and rust-eaten, arm-bracelets many,
Artfully woven.   Wealth can easily,
Gold on the sea-bottom, turn into vanity [1]
15 Each one of earthmen, arm him who pleaseth !
And he saw there lying an all-golden banner
High o'er the hoard, of hand-wonders greatest,
Linkèd with lacets: a light from it sparkled,
That the floor of the cavern he was able to look on,
20 To examine the jewels.   Sight of the dragon

Wiglaf fulfils his lord's behest.

The dragon's den.

The dragon is not there.

[1] The word 'oferhígian' (2767) being vague and little understood, two quite distinct translations of this passage have arisen. One takes 'oferhígian' as meaning 'to exceed,' and, inserting 'hord' after 'gehwone,' renders: *The treasure may easily, the gold in the ground, exceed in value every hoard of man, hide it who will.* The other takes 'oferhígian' as meaning 'to render arrogant,' and, giving the sentence a moralizing tone, renders substantially as in the body of this work. (Cf. 28₁₃ et seq.)

Not any was offered, but edge off-carried him.

Wiglaf bears the
hoard away.

Then I heard that the hero the hoard-treasure plundered,
The giant-work ancient reaved in the cavern,
Bare on his bosom the beakers and platters,
25 As himself would fain have it, and took off the standard,
The brightest of beacons ;[1] the bill had erst injured
(Its edge was of iron), the old-ruler's weapon,
Him who long had watched as ward of the jewels,
Who fire-terror carried hot for the treasure,
30 Rolling in battle, in middlemost darkness,
Till murdered he perished.   The messenger hastened,
Not loth to return, hurried by jewels :
Curiosity urged him if, excellent-mooded,
Alive he should find the lord of the Weders
35 Mortally wounded, at the place where he left him.
'Mid the jewels he found then the famous old chieftain,
His liegelord belovèd, at his life's-end gory :
He thereupon 'gan to lave him with water,
Till the point of his word piercèd his breast-hoard.
40 Beowulf spake (the gold-gems he noticed),

Beowulf is rejoiced
to see the jewels.

The old one in sorrow : " For the jewels I look on
Thanks do I utter for all to the Ruler,
Wielder of Worship, with words of devotion,
The Lord everlasting, that He let me such treasures
45 Gain for my people ere death overtook me.
Since I've bartered the agèd life to me granted
For treasure of jewels, attend ye henceforward

He desires to be
held in memory by
his people.

The wants of the war-thanes ; I can wait here no longer.
The battle-famed bid ye to build them a grave-hill,
50 Bright when I'm burned, at the brim-current's limit ;
As a memory-mark to the men I have governed,

---

[1] The passage beginning here is very much disputed. 'The bill of the old
lord' is by some regarded as Beowulf's sword; by others, as that of the
ancient possessor of the hoard. ' Ǽr gescód ' (2778), translated in this work
as verb and adverb, is by some regarded as a compound participial adj. =
sheathed in brass.

Aloft it shall tower on Whale's-Ness uprising,
That earls of the ocean hereafter may call it
Beowulf's barrow, those who barks ever-dashing
55 From a distance shall drive o'er the darkness of waters."
The bold-mooded troop-lord took from his neck then
The ring that was golden, gave to his liegeman,
The youthful war-hero, his gold-flashing helmet,
His collar and war-mail, bade him well to enjoy them :
60 " Thou art latest left of the line of our kindred,
Of Wægmunding people : Weird hath offcarried
All of my kinsmen to the Creator's glory,
Earls in their vigor : I shall after them fare."
'Twas the agèd liegelord's last-spoken word in
65 His musings of spirit, ere he mounted the fire,
The battle-waves burning : from his bosom departed
His soul to seek the sainted ones' glory.

XXXIX.

THE DEAD FOES. — WIGLAF'S BITTER TAUNTS.

It had wofully chanced then the youthful retainer
To behold on earth the most ardent-belovèd
At his life-days' limit, lying there helpless.
The slayer too lay there, of life all bereavèd,
5 Horrible earth-drake, harassed with sorrow :
The round-twisted monster was permitted no longer
To govern the ring-hoards, but edges of war-swords
Mightily seized him, battle-sharp, sturdy
Leavings of hammers, that still from his wounds
10 The flier-from-farland fell to the earth
Hard by his hoard-house, hopped he at midnight
Not e'er through the air, nor exulting in jewels
Suffered them to see him : but he sank then to earthward
Through the hero-chief's handwork. I heard sure it throve
   then

15 But few in the land of liegemen of valor,
Though of every achievement bold he had proved him,
To run 'gainst the breath of the venomous scather,
Or the hall of the treasure to trouble with hand-blows,
If he watching had found the ward of the hoard-hall
20 On the barrow abiding. Beowulf's part of
The treasure of jewels was paid for with death ;
Each of the twain had attained to the end of
Life so unlasting.   Not long was the time till

The tardy-at-battle returned from the thicket,
25 The timid truce-breakers ten all together,
Who durst not before play with the lances
In the prince of the people's pressing emergency ;

But blushing with shame, with shields they betook them,
With arms and armor where the old one was lying :
30 They gazed upon Wiglaf.   He was sitting exhausted,
Foot-going fighter, not far from the shoulders
Of the lord of the people, would rouse him with water:
No whit did it help him ; though he hoped for it keenly,
He was able on earth not at all in the leader
35 Life to retain, and nowise to alter
The will of the Wielder ; the World-Ruler's power [1]
Would govern the actions of each one of heroes,

As yet He is doing.   From the young one forthwith then
Could grim-worded greeting be got for him quickly
40 Whose courage had failed him.   Wiglaf discoursed then,
Weohstan his son, sad-mooded hero,

Looked on the hated : " He who soothness will utter
Can say that the liegelord who gave you the jewels,
The ornament-armor wherein ye are standing,
45 When on ale-bench often he offered to hall-men
Helmet and burnie, the prince to his liegemen,
As best upon earth he was able to find him, —

---

[1] For ' dædum rædan ' (2859) B. suggests ' déañ áréðan,' and renders: *The
might (or judgment) of God would determine death for every man, as he still
does.*

That he wildly wasted his war-gear undoubtedly
When battle o'ertook him.[1] The troop-king no need had
50 To glory in comrades ; yet God permitted him,
Victory-Wielder, with weapon unaided
Himself to avenge, when vigor was needed.
1 life-protection but little was able
To give him in battle, and I 'gan, notwithstanding,
55 Helping my kinsman (my strength overtaxing) :
He waxed the weaker when with weapon I smote on
My mortal opponent, the fire less strongly
Flamed from his bosom. Too few of protectors
Came round the king at the critical moment.
60 Now must ornament-taking and weapon-bestowing,
Home-joyance all, cease for your kindred,
Food for the people ; each of your warriors
Must needs be bereavèd of rights that he holdeth
In landed possessions, when faraway nobles
65 Shall learn of your leaving your lord so basely,
The dastardly deed. Death is more pleasant
To every earlman than infamous life is ! "

Surely our lord wasted his armor on poltroons.

He, however, got along without you.

With some aid, I could have saved our liegelord.

Gift-giving is over with your people: the ring-lord is dead.

What is life without honor?

XL.

THE MESSENGER OF DEATH.

Then he charged that the battle be announced at the hedge
Up o'er the cliff-edge, where the earl-troopers bided
The whole of the morning, mood-wretched sat them,
Bearers of battle-shields, both things expecting,
5 The end of his lifetime and the coming again of
The liegelord belovèd. Little reserved he
Of news that was known, who the ness-cliff did travel,
But he truly discoursed to all that could hear him :

Wiglaf sends the news of Beowulf's death to liegemen near by.

---

[1] Some critics, H. himself in earlier editions, put the clause, ' When . . .
him ' (A.-S. ' þá . . . begct') with the following sentence; that is, they make it
dependent upon ' þorfte ' (2875) instead of upon ' forwurpe ' (2873).

The messenger speaks.

" Now the free-giving friend-lord of the folk of the Weders,
10 The folk-prince of Geatmen, is fast in his death-bed,
By the deeds of the dragon in death-bed abideth ;
Along with him lieth his life-taking foeman
Slain with knife-wounds : he was wholly unable
To injure at all the ill-planning monster

Wiglaf sits by our dead lord.

15 With bite of his sword-edge. Wiglaf is sitting,
Offspring of Wihstan, up over Beowulf,
Earl o'er another whose end-day hath reached him,
Head-watch holdeth o'er heroes unliving,[1]

Our lord's death will lead to attacks from our old foes.

For friend and for foeman. The folk now expecteth
20 A season of strife when the death of the folk-king
To Frankmen and Frisians in far-lands is published.

Higelac's death recalled.

The war-hatred waxed warm 'gainst the Hugmen,
When Higelac came with an army of vessels
Faring to Friesland, where the Frankmen in battle
25 Humbled him and bravely with overmight 'complished
That the mail-clad warrior must sink in the battle,
Fell 'mid his folk-troop : no fret-gems presented
The atheling to earlmen ; aye was denied us
Merewing's mercy. The men of the Swedelands
30 For truce or for truth trust I but little ;
But widely 'twas known that near Ravenswood Ongentheow

Hæthcyn's fall referred to.

Sundered Hæthcyn the Hrethling from life-joys,
When for pride overweening the War-Scylfings first did
Seek the Geatmen with savage intentions.
35 Early did Ohthere's age-laden father,
Old and terrible, give blow in requital,
Killing the sea-king, the queen-mother rescued,
The old one his consort deprived of her gold,
Onela's mother and Ohthere's also,

---

[1] ' Hige-méðum ' (2910) is glossed by H. as dat. plu. (= for the dead). S. proposes ' hige-méðe,' nom. sing. limiting Wígláf; i.e. *W., mood-weary, holds head-watch o'er friend and foe.* — B. suggests taking the word as dat. inst. plu. of an abstract noun in -' u.' The translation would be substantially the same as S.'s.

40 And then followed the feud-nursing foemen till hardly,
Reaved of their ruler, they Ravenswood entered.
Then with vast-numbered forces he assaulted the remnant,
Weary with wounds, woe often promised
The livelong night to the sad-hearted war-troop :
45 Said he at morning would kill them with edges of weapons,
Some on the gallows for glee to the fowls.
Aid came after to the anxious-in-spirit
At dawn of the day, after Higelac's bugle
And trumpet-sound heard they, when the good one proceeded
50 And faring followed the flower of the troopers.

XLI.

THE MESSENGER'S RETROSPECT.

"The blood-stainèd trace of Swedes and Geatmen,
The death-rush of warmen, widely was noticed,
How the folks with each other feud did awaken.
The worthy one went then[1] with well-beloved comrades,
5 Old and dejected to go to the fastness,
Ongentheo earl upward then turned him ;
Of Higelac's battle he'd heard on inquiry,
The exultant one's prowess, despaired of resistance,
With earls of the ocean to be able to struggle,
10 'Gainst sea-going sailors to save the hoard-treasure,
His wife and his children ; he fled after thenceward
Old 'neath the earth-wall.   Then was offered pursuance
To the braves of the Swedemen, the banner[2] to Higelac.

The messenger
continues, and
refers to the feuds
of Swedes and
Geats.

[1] For 'góda,' which seems a surprising epithet for a Geat to apply to the
"terrible" Ongentheow, B. suggests 'gomela.'   The passage would then
stand : ' The old one went then,' etc.

[2] For 'segn Higeláce,' K., Th., and B. propose 'segn Higeláces,' meaning :
Higelac's banner followed the Swedes (in pursuit). — S. suggests 'sæcc Higeláces,' and renders : Higelac's pursuit. — The H.-So. reading, as translated in
our text, means that the banner of the enemy was captured and brought to
Higelac as a trophy.

They fared then forth o'er the field-of-protection,

15 When the Hrethling heroes hedgeward had thronged them.
Then with edges of irons was Ongentheow driven,
The gray-haired to tarry, that the troop-ruler had to
Suffer the power solely of Eofor:

Wulf then wildly with weapon assaulted him,

20 Wonred his son, that for swinge of the edges
The blood from his body burst out in currents,
Forth 'neath his hair.   He feared not however,
Gray-headed Scylfing, but speedily quited

The wasting wound-stroke with worse exchange,

25 When the king of the thane-troop thither did turn him:
The wise-mooded son of Wonred was powerless
To give a return-blow to the age-hoary man,
But his head-shielding helmet first hewed he to pieces,
That fleckèd with gore perforce he did totter,

30 Fell to the earth; not fey was he yet then,
But up did he spring though an edge-wound had reached him.

Then Higelac's vassal, valiant and dauntless,
When his brother lay dead, made his broad-bladed weapon,
Giant-sword ancient, defence of the giants,

35 Bound o'er the shield-wall; the folk-prince succumbed then,

Shepherd of people, was pierced to the vitals.
There were many attendants who bound up his kinsman,
Carried him quickly when occasion was granted
That the place of the slain they were suffered to manage.

40 This pending, one hero plundered the other,
His armor of iron from Ongentheow ravished,
His hard-sword hilted and helmet together;

The old one's equipments he carried to Higelac.
He the jewels received, and rewards 'mid the troopers

45 Graciously promised, and so did accomplish:
The king of the Weders requited the war-rush,
Hrethel's descendant, when home he repaired him,

To Eofor and Wulf with wide-lavished treasures,
To each of them granted a hundred of thousands

50 In land and rings wrought out of wire :
None upon mid-earth needed to twit him [1]
With the gifts he gave them, when glory they conquered ;
And to Eofor then gave he his one only daughter,
The honor of home, as an earnest of favor.
55 That's the feud and hatred — as ween I 'twill happen —
The anger of earthmen, that earls of the Swedemen
Will visit on us, when they hear that our leader
Lifeless is lying, he who longtime protected
His hoard and kingdom 'gainst hating assailers,
60 Who on the fall of the heroes defended of yore
The deed-mighty Scyldings,[2] did for the troopers
What best did avail them, and further moreover
Hero-deeds 'complished.   Now is haste most fitting,
That the lord of liegemen we look upon yonder,
65 And *that* one carry on journey to death-pyre
Who ring-presents gave us.   Not aught of it all
Shall melt with the brave one — there's a mass of bright jewels,
Gold beyond measure, grewsomely purchased
And ending it all ornament-rings too
70 Bought with his life ; these fire shall devour,
Flame shall cover, no earlman shall wear
A jewel-memento, nor beautiful virgin
Have on her neck rings to adorn her,
But wretched in spirit bereavèd of gold-gems
75 She shall oft with others be exiled and banished,
Since the leader of liegemen hath laughter forsaken,

His gifts were beyond cavil.

To Eofor he also gives his only daughter in marriage.

It is time for us to pay the last marks of respect to our lord.

[1] The rendering given in this translation represents the king as being generous beyond the possibility of reproach; but some authorities construe 'him' (2996) as plu., and understand the passage to mean that no one reproached the two brothers with having received more reward than they were entitled to.

[2] The name 'Scyldingas' here (3006) has caused much discussion, and given rise to several theories, the most important of which are as follows: (1) After the downfall of Hrothgar's family, Beowulf was king of the Danes, or Scyldings. (2) For 'Scyldingas' read 'Scylfingas' — that is, after killing Eadgils, the Scylfing prince, Beowulf conquered his land, and held it in subjection. (3) M. considers 3006 a thoughtless repetition of 2053.   (Cf. H.-So.)

Mirth and merriment. Hence many a war-spear
Cold from the morning shall be clutched in the fingers,
Heaved in the hand, no harp-music's sound shall
80 Waken the warriors, but the wan-coated raven
Fain over fey ones freely shall gabble,
Shall say to the eagle how he sped in the eating,
When, the wolf his companion, he plundered the slain."
So the high-minded hero was rehearsing these stories
85 Loathsóme to hear ; he lied as to few of

The warriors go
sadly to look at
Beowulf's lifeless
body.

Weirds and of words.   All the war-troop arose then,
'Neath the Eagle's Cape sadly betook them,
Weeping and woful, the wonder to look at.
They saw on the sand then soulless a-lying,
90 His slaughter-bed holding, him who rings had given them
In days that were done ; then the death-bringing moment
Was come to the good one, that the king very warlike,
Wielder of Weders, with wonder-death perished.
First they beheld there a creature more wondrous,

They also see the
dragon.

95 The worm on the field, in front of them lying,
The foeman before them : the fire-spewing dragon,
Ghostly and grisly guest in his terrors,
Was scorched in the fire ; as he lay there he measured
Fifty of feet ; came forth in the night-time [1]
100 To rejoice in the air, thereafter departing
To visit his den ; he in death was then fastened,
He would joy in no other earth-hollowed caverns.
There stood round about him beakers and vessels,
Dishes were lying and dear-valued weapons,
105 With iron-rust eaten, as in earth's mighty bosom
A thousand of winters there they had rested :

The hoard was
under a magic
spell.

That mighty bequest then with magic was guarded,
Gold of the ancients, that earlman not any
The ring-hall could touch, save Ruling-God only,

---

[1] B. takes ' nihtes' and ' hwílum' (3045) as separate adverbial cases, and renders: *Joy in the air had he of yore by night, etc.* He thinks that the idea of vanished time ought to be expressed.

110 Sooth-king of Vict'ries gave whom He wished to
[1] (He is earth-folk's protector) to open the treasure,
E'en to such among mortals as seemed to Him proper.

God alone could
give access to it.

XLII.

WIGLAF'S SAD STORY. — THE HOARD CARRIED OFF.

Then 'twas seen that the journey prospered him little
Who wrongly within had the ornaments hidden [2]
Down 'neath the wall. The warden erst slaughtered
Some few of the folk-troop: the feud then thereafter
5 Was hotly avengèd. 'Tis a wonder where,[3]
When the strength-famous trooper has attained to the end of
Life-days allotted, then no longer the man may
Remain with his kinsmen where mead-cups are flowing.
So to Beowulf happened when the ward of the barrow,
10 Assaults, he sought for: himself had no knowledge
How his leaving this life was likely to happen.
So to doomsday, famous folk-leaders down did
Call it with curses — who 'complished it there —

---

[1] The parenthesis is by some emended so as to read: (1) (*He* (i.e. *God*)
is the hope of men); (2) (*he is the hope of heroes*). Gr.'s reading has no
parenthesis, but says: . . . *could touch, unless God himself, true king of victo-
ries, gave to whom he would to open the treasure, the secret place of enchanters,
etc.* The last is rejected on many grounds.

[2] For 'gehýdde,' B. suggests 'gehýðde': the passage would stand as above
except the change of 'hidden' (v. 2) to 'plundered.' The reference, however, would be to the thief, not to the dragon.

[3] The passage 'Wundur . . . búan' (3063-3066), M. took to be a question
asking whether it was strange that a man should die when his appointed time
had come. — B. sees a corruption, and makes emendations introducing the
idea that a brave man should not die from sickness or from old age, but should
find death in the performance of some deed of daring. — S. sees an indirect
question introduced by 'hwár' and dependent upon 'wundur': *A secret is it
when the hero is to die, etc.* — Why may the two clauses not be parallel, and
the whole passage an Old English cry of '*How wonderful is death!*'? — S.'s
is the best yet offered, if 'wundor' means 'mystery.'

That that man should be ever of ill-deeds convicted,
15 Confined in foul-places, fastened in hell-bonds,
Punished with plagues, who this place should e'er ravage.[1]
He cared not for gold : rather the Wielder's
Favor preferred he first to get sight of.[2]

*Wiglaf addresses
his comrades.*

Wiglaf discoursed then, Wihstan his son :
20 " Oft many an earlman on one man's account must
Sorrow endure, as to us it hath happened.
The liegelord belovèd we could little prevail on,
Kingdom's keeper, counsel to follow,
Not to go to the guardian of the gold-hoard, but let him
25 Lie where he long was, live in his dwelling
Till the end of the world.   Met we a destiny
Hard to endure : the hoard has been looked at,
Been gained very grimly ; too grievous the fate that[3]
The prince of the people pricked to come thither.
30 *I* was therein and all of it looked at,
The building's equipments, since access was given me,
Not kindly at all entrance permitted

*He tells them of
Beowulf's last
moments.*

Within under earth-wall.   Hastily seized I
And held in my hands a huge-weighing burden
35 Of hoard-treasures costly, hither out bare them
To my liegelord belovèd : life was yet in him,
And consciousness also ; the old one discoursed then
Much and mournfully, commanded to greet you,

*Beowulf's dying
request.*

Bade that remembering the deeds of your friend-lord
40 Ye build on the fire-hill of corpses a lofty
Burial-barrow, broad and far-famous,
As 'mid world-dwelling warriors he was widely most honored
While he reveled in riches.   Let us rouse us and hasten

---

[1] For 'strude' in H.-So., S. suggests 'stride.' This would require 'ravage'
(v. 16) to be changed to 'tread.'
[2] 'He cared . . . sight of' (17, 18), S. emends so as to read as follows:
He (Beowulf) had not before seen the favor of the avaricious possessor.
[3] B. renders: *That which drew the king thither* (i.e. *the treasure*) *was
granted us, but in such a way that it overcomes us.*

Again to see and seek for the treasure,
45 The wonder 'neath wall. The way I will show you,
That close ye may look at ring-gems sufficient
And gold in abundance. Let the bier with promptness
Fully be fashioned, when forth we shall come,
And lift we our lord, then, where long he shall tarry,
50 Well-beloved warrior, 'neath the Wielder's protection."
Then the son of Wihstan bade orders be given,

Wiglaf charges them to build a funeral-pyre.

Mood-valiant man, to many of heroes,
Holders of homesteads, that they hither from far,
¹ Leaders of liegemen, should look for the good one
55 With wood for his pyre : "The flame shall now swallow
(The wan fire shall wax²) the warriors' leader
Who the rain of the iron often abided,
When, sturdily hurled, the storm of the arrows
Leapt o'er linden-wall, the lance rendered service,
60 Furnished with feathers followed the arrow."
Now the wise-mooded son of Wihstan did summon
The best of the braves from the band of the ruler
Seven together; 'neath the enemy's roof he
Went with the seven ; one of the heroes

He takes seven thanes, and enters the den.

65 Who fared at the front, a fire-blazing torch-light
Bare in his hand. No lot then decided
Who that hoard should havoc, when hero-earls saw it
Lying in the cavern uncared-for entirely,
Rusting to ruin : they rued then but little
70 That they hastily hence hauled out the treasure,
The dear-valued jewels ; the dragon eke pushed they,
The worm o'er the wall, let the wave-currents take him,

They push the dragon over the wall.

---

¹ 'Folc-ágende' (3114) B. takes as dat. sing. with 'gódum,' and refers it to Beowulf; that is, *Should bring fire-wood to the place where the good folk-ruler lay.*

² C. proposes to take 'weaxan' = L. 'vescor,' and translate *devour.* This gives a parallel to 'fretan' above. The parenthesis would be discarded and the passage read: *Now shall the fire consume, the wan-flame devour, the prince of warriors, etc.*

The waters enwind the ward of the treasures.

The hoard is laid
on a wain.
There wounden gold on a wain was uploaded,

75 A mass unmeasured, the men-leader off then,

The hero hoary, to Whale's-Ness was carried.

XLIII.

THE BURNING OF BEOWULF.

Beowulf's pyre.
The folk of the Geatmen got him then ready

A pile on the earth strong for the burning,

Behung with helmets, hero-knights' targets,

And bright-shining burnies, as he begged they should have them;

5 Then wailing war-heroes their world-famous chieftain,

Their liegelord belovèd, laid in the middle.

The funeral-flame.
Soldiers began then to make on the barrow

The largest of dead-fires: dark o'er the vapor

The smoke-cloud ascended, the sad-roaring fire,

10 Mingled with weeping (the wind-roar subsided)

Till the building of bone it had broken to pieces,

Hot in the heart. Heavy in spirit

They mood-sad lamented the men-leader's ruin;

And mournful measures the much-grieving widow

15 * * * * * * *

 * * * * * * *

 * * * * * * *

 * * * * * * *

 * * * * * * *

20 * * * * * * *

The Weders carry
out their lord's last
request.
The men of the Weders made accordingly

A hill on the height, high and extensive,

Of sea-going sailors to be seen from a distance,

And the brave one's beacon built where the fire was,

25 In ten-days' space, with a wall surrounded it,

As wisest of world-folk could most worthily plan it.

They placed in the barrow rings and jewels,

All such ornaments as erst in the treasure
War-mooded men had won in possession :

30 The earnings of earlmen to earth they entrusted,
The gold to the dust, where yet it remaineth
As useless to mortals as in foregoing eras.
'Round the dead-mound rode then the doughty-in-battle,
Bairns of all twelve of the chiefs of the people,

35 More would they mourn, lament for their ruler,
Speak in measure, mention him with pleasure,
Weighed his worth, and his warlike achievements
Mightily commended, as 'tis meet one praise his
Liegelord in words and love him in spirit,

40 When forth from his body he fares to destruction.
So lamented mourning the men of the Geats,
Fond-loving vassals, the fall of their lord,
Said he was gentlest of kings under heaven,
Mildest of men and most philanthropic,

45 Friendliest to folk-troops and fondest of honor.

Rings and gems
are laid in the
barrow.

They mourn for
their lord, and sing
his praises.

An ideal king.

ADDENDA.

SEVERAL discrepancies and other oversights have been noticed in the H.-So. glossary. Of these a good part were avoided by Harrison and Sharp, the American editors of Beowulf, in their last edition, 1888. The rest will, I hope, be noticed in their fourth edition. As, however, this book may fall into the hands of some who have no copy of the American edition, it seems best to notice all the principal oversights of the German editors.

From hám (194). — Notes and glossary conflict; the latter not having been altered to suit the conclusions accepted in the former.

þær gelýfan sceal dryhtnes dóme (440). — Under 'dóm' H. says 'the might of the Lord'; while under 'gelýfan' he says 'the judgment of the Lord.'

Eal bencþelu (486). — Under 'benc-þelu' H. says *nom. plu.;* while under 'eal' he says *nom. sing.*

Heatho-ræmas (519). — Under 'ætberan' H. translates 'to the Heathoremes'; while under 'Heatho-ræmas' he says 'Heathorœmas reaches Breca in the swimming-match with Beowulf.' Harrison and Sharp (3d edition, 1888) avoid the discrepancy.

Fáh féond-scaða (554). — Under 'féond-scaða' H. says 'a gleaming sea-monster'; under 'fáh' he says 'hostile.'

Onfeng hraðe inwit-þancum (749). — Under 'onfón' H. says 'he *received* the maliciously-disposed one'; under 'inwit-þanc' he says 'he *grasped*,' etc.

Nið-wundor séon (1366). — Under 'nið-wundor' H. calls this word itself *nom. sing.;* under 'séon' he translates it as accus. sing., understanding 'man' as subject of 'séon.' H. and S. (3d edition) make the correction.

Forgeaf hilde-bille (1521). — H., under the second word, calls it instr. dat.; while under 'forgifan' he makes it the dat. of indir. obj. H. and S. (3d edition) make the change.

Brád and **brún-ecg** (1547). — Under 'brád' H. says 'das breite Hüftmesser mit bronzener Klinge'; under 'brún-ecg' he says 'ihr breites Hüftmesser mit blitzender Klinge.'

Ȳðelíce (1557). — Under this word H. makes it modify 'ástód.' If this be right, the punctuation of the fifth edition is wrong. See H. and S., appendix.

Sélran gesóhtc (1840). — Under 'sél' and 'gesécan' H. calls these two words accus. plu.; but this is clearly an error, as both are nom. plu., pred. nom. H. and S. correct under 'sél.'

Wið sylfne (1978). — Under 'wið' and 'gesittan' H. says 'wið = near, by'; under 'self' he says 'opposite.'

þéow (2225) is omitted from the glossary.

For duguðum (2502). — Under 'duguð' H. translates this phrase, 'in Tüchtigkeit'; under 'for,' by 'vor der edlen Kriegerschaar.'

þær (2574). — Under 'wealdan' H. translates *þær* by 'wo'; under 'mótan,' by 'da.' H. and S. suggest 'if' in both passages.

Wunde (2726). — Under 'wund' H. says 'dative,' and under 'wæl-bléate' he says 'accus.' It is without doubt accus., parallel with 'benne.'

Strengum gebæded (3118). — Under 'strengo' H. says 'Strengum' = mit Macht; under 'gebæded' he translates 'von den Sehnen.' H. and S. correct this discrepancy by rejecting the second reading.

Bronda be láfe (3162). — A recent emendation. The fourth edition had 'bronda betost.' In the fifth edition the editor neglects to change the glossary to suit the new emendation. See 'bewyrcan.'

BIOGRAPHICAL SKETCH.

I was born in Richmond, Va., on Mar. 2, 1856. At an early age, I was entered at the University School, which for twenty-five years occupied a high position among the academies of Virginia. There I remained four years under the instruction of several men honorably known among teachers of the South. My English studies I began under Mr. Thos. R. Price, now of Columbia College, N.Y., and Maj. Innes Randolph, late of the Baltimore American. From that school I went to Randolph Macon College. There again I studied under Prof. T. R. Price, catching his enthusiasm for English studies. On acount of serious trouble with my eyes, I had to leave college without a degree ; but the session and a half spent at Randolph Macon College served to deepen my inborn love for books. In 1873, I entered mercantile life. After some years, however, my literary tastes drove me out of pursuits so uncongenial. Then I became a teacher. After four years experience in the school-room, I determined to fit myself for a college chair. I accordingly entered the Johns Hopkins University, choosing English as my principal subject, with German and History as subsidiary subjects. There I studied from Oct., 1885, to June, 1888, under Doctors Bright, Wood, Adams, and Bloomfield, the last named scholar giving me Comparative Philology. To all these gentlemen I am indebted for many courtesies and for inspiration. In 1886–1887 I had the honor of being Fellow in English.

J. L. HALL.

WIILLIAMSBURG, VA., June 10, 1892.

www.ingramcontent.com/pod-product-compliance
Lightning Source LLC
Chambersburg PA
CBHW020409030726
47496CB00007B/2380